To Richard, Miranda, and Nathaniel

Well Wished

Franny Billingsley

A JEAN KARL BOOK

ALADDIN PAPERBACKS

New York   London   Toronto   Sydney   Singapore

First Aladdin Paperbacks edition February 2000

Aladdin Paperbacks
An imprint of Simon & Schuster
Children's Publishing Division
1230 Avenue of the Americas
New York, NY 10020

The Library of Congress has cataloged the hardcover edition as follows:
Billingsley, Franny.
Well wished / by Franny Billingsley.—1st ed.
p. cm.
"A Jean Karl book."
Summary: In a time of dire need, eleven-year-old Nuria tries to outwit the magical wishing well in her mysterious mountain village.
ISBN 0-689-81210-8 (hc.)
[1. Wishes—Fiction. 2. Magic— Fiction. 3. Fantasy.] I.Title.
PZ7.B4985We   1997
[Fic]—dc20
96-24511
ISBN 0-689-83255-9 (Aladdin pbk.)

Contents

The Avy's Wish

It was on a winter afternoon, just before Christmas, that Nuria finally gave up the idea of making a wish. She stood on the embankment that bounded the village Common and looked at the Wishing Well. It didn't even tempt her. Then she gazed about her with pleasure. More than a year had passed since she'd come to live with her grandfather in Bishop Mayne, but it was still hard to believe she lived in such a beautiful place.

The trees stood black and sleek as skeletons, their crisp edges blurred to velvet by the failing light. But there was nothing blurred about the Wishing Well, which rose from the pale winter grass in a massive sweep of granite. Agnes, the Well's Guardian, was a mere shadow beside it, knitting as she rocked in the great stone chair, rocking and knitting just as each Guardian had done for as long as anyone could remember.

Nuria snapped her fingers high into the air. She liked the bright, brave sound it made. "Danger is as nothing to Nuria, the undaunted," she said, for when she came to Bishop Mayne last year, her grandfather, the Avy, had told her first thing that the Well was dangerous and she must set out of her mind the idea of wishing.

A great black dog with pointed ears and yellow eyes nudged the back of her leg. Osa was officially the Avy's dog, but she'd attached herself to Nuria when Nuria arrived last year, trailing her now so closely and constantly that the Avy sometimes laughed and said Osa knew who really was in charge.

"Patience, noble wolf!" said Nuria. "Before we approach, let the Guardian of the Well speak."

"A coin for passage to your heart's desire," said Agnes. "That is the first rule."

Nuria sprang suddenly down the embankment, her empty hands thrown behind her for balance. "I'll beat you to the Well, Osa!" she said. She wore one gray mitten and one green, but it was a wonder she had any mittens on at all, and since no hat could be persuaded to stay on her head for more than two minutes, wild drifts of coppery hair flew behind her as she ran. Osa trailed her like a shadow.

"One wish each lifetime," said Agnes. "One cycle of the moon to repent and call it back. That is the second rule."

Nuria slapped the cold granite wall. "Ha! I won!" she declared, petting Osa, who dissolved into a puddle of bliss, leaning heavily against her. Melting, Nuria called it. Nuria let Osa melt into her leg and watched the light snow sparkle into the pools of lamplight in the village Square. These were both calming things, but Nuria was not calm inside.

Just that morning, the Avy had wished for the only thing Nuria wanted anymore. Nothing had happened, not yet, but Agnes might know if the wish would come true. Nuria put on her impatient face, the one most grown-ups hated. "Just get on with it," she muttered, because Agnes couldn't say anything until she'd recited the last rule of the Well. Nuria's words came to life in a chilly cloud that hung in front of her mouth, then vanished.

"And for that cycle of the moon your lips are locked in this: To no one may you speak of your wish. To no one but to me, for your wish is my wish too. That is the third rule."

Now that the time had come for her to ask, Nuria was suddenly afraid. What if the Avy's wish hadn't come true? A friend was the only thing she wanted in the whole world, except for someone who loved her just the way she was, and that wish had come true the moment she met the Avy.

She'd always wanted a friend, even when she lived with Aunt Hortense and hadn't known there was an Avy. She never played with her cousins, who wanted her to be a proper orphan, quiet and timid and grateful they'd taken her in. But Nuria was not grateful, and anything quiet was impossible for her, so she'd always been alone.

"I know the Avy's wish isn't just for me," she said, repeating what the Avy had told her so often. He wanted her to understand he had to make a wish for the whole village. Everyone wanted to undo that other wish—that terrible wish—that had made all the children disappear. "But if the children do get wished back, I hope there will be one special friend for me."

The great stone chair creaked, rocking along the deep ruts that decades, centuries, of Guardians had worn into the ground. "Do you have a coin?" said Agnes. "The Well gets hungry so quickly these days."

Nuria looked at Agnes with dislike. "You won't get me to make a wish." Agnes was wrapped as always in a harlequin collection of shawls and skirts, and she was so old that even the Avy couldn't guess her age, for time had dropped over her a veil of fine lines like ancient lace.

"I wouldn't use up my only wish!" said Nuria. "And if I did, I'd be careful how I said it. I wouldn't need to take it back, not like him."

She pointed to a granite pillar that stood about twenty feet from the Well. It resembled a man in height and breadth, narrowing decidedly near the top, then swelling into a rounded lump that peered over its shoulder at Agnes. On this lump were curves and hollows that might once have been cheeks and jaws and temples. There were two dark pits that might once have been eyes.

"I'd never wish to be a *pillar of society*," said Nuria with contempt. "What an idiotic wish. The Well must have thought so too, turning that man into a pillar."

"If you have no wish for me," said Agnes, "what is your business here today?"

"Did the Avy's wish come true?" Nuria held out her hands, palms up, to show how empty they were. "I've wanted a friend for so long, and Bishop Mayne must be the only place in the world with no other children."

It hadn't always been that way, though. The village had been full of children when Nuria arrived last year. But she hadn't even had a chance to meet anyone before . . . Well, no one knew exactly what had happened on that dreadful day. It started at midnight with the screaming, followed by the sudden silence, which was even worse. The children's beds were empty by the time the parents could reach them, although the sheets were still warm. All the children disappeared except Nuria in her mountaintop cottage, and also one other girl, whose father took her away the very next morning. For her health, he said.

The Avy had explained it as best he could to Nuria. The Well was to blame, naturally. Some plaguey fool had made a wish, and as usual the wish had gone wrong. And even though the children had been found, no one dared bring them back again, and so the parents had left too.

"The Avy's the bravest one of all," said Nuria. "That's why they asked him to make a wish for the families to come back."

"Brave or foolish, take your pick," said Agnes, and drew a spiraling tendril of white smoke from a basket at her feet. She began to cast it onto one of her knitting needles.

Nuria stepped back. Usually the Guardian's smoke creations vanished into the air. But sometimes they didn't, and Nuria had a vague understanding that this meant trouble, although she didn't know what kind of trouble it might be.

"What are you knitting?" said Nuria, watching the white smoke spin from Agnes's needles, growing and taking shape, settling now into the size and form of a faceless head.

"Here's your answer," said Agnes. Her needles trembled, and the globe of smoke shifted. It drew into itself in places, curved out in others, and settled finally into the head of a young girl. Agnes curled a tendril of green smoke round her needle, and a moment later the face was staring at Nuria with glowing green eyes.

"Here is the result of the Avy's wish," said Agnes, and cast the last loop of smoke off the needle. The face hung bodiless, swaying slightly in the restless air. "Meet the first child to return. Catty Winter is eleven years old, just like you. She and her father have already returned to the old Winter place—have already been deposited there, I should say."

Catty! Nuria tried to speak, but she was breathless and trembling and could make no sound. Her heart skittered ahead of her body, and she had to run around the Well to catch up with it. Osa followed, barking and nipping at Nuria's heels.

"The families are coming back!" cried Nuria. "And there's a special friend for me!"

Agnes put her hands to her ears. "Don't imagine that because I cannot feel I also cannot hear."

"The Avy says I'm too loud," agreed Nuria cheerfully, ignoring this reminder of the Well's heavy-handed ways. It had fixed things so that its Guardians, bound as they were to the chair, day and night, in rain and sun and snow, could feel nothing at all. It was probably to protect the Guardians, but Nuria thought she'd rather die than be protected like that. She hoisted herself onto the Well and leaned into it from her stomach.

"Clever Avy!" she shouted. "He made the wish come true. Oh clever, clever Avy!"

"Avy," said the Well in its hollow echo. "Avy . . . Avy . . . Avy . . ."

Nuria's eyes hadn't adjusted to the twilight inside the Well, and she took a deep breath to smell the roses that bloomed on the granite walls. She heard the hummingbirds in flight, strumming the fragrant air with their wings. The Avy said that the Well's everlasting spring must somehow leak into the surrounding landscape, for certainly Bishop Mayne was the most fertile and beautiful place anywhere in the region. Winter was short, and spring and summer long. Sweet corn grew from April to November, and the strawberries were as big as Nuria's hand.

Then, as Nuria's eyes began to work, a nightingale emerged, a small patch of gray against the darker granite. The hummingbirds' eggs were specks of light in the woven cup of their nest, none of them bigger than the tip of Nuria's little finger. Nuria peered down to the water below, but it was too dark to send back even a glimmer of pale skin and coppery hair.

"Do you think my new friend will like the way I look? Maybe I should wish for long, sooty lashes."

"You'll need a coin to make a wish," said Agnes.

"I'm not an idiot. In all the fairy stories, if you wish for beauty, you end up with toads in your mouth. But it's just that I'm so plain. Look at how big my mouth is! And these lashes!"

She hated her long, light lashes, which disappeared on a cloudy day, giving her the look of an old-fashioned portrait, pale and serene with high, flat cheekbones and long, naked eyes. The Avy always told her that her great gray eyes were beautiful, and that he loved their flecks of gold. Gold stars, he called them. And now, thinking of the Avy, Nuria slipped to the ground. She had to tell him the news.

"Winding up," she said, swinging her arms in wide circles and springing across the grass and up the embankment. The cobblestones in the village Square were slippery with snow, but on she ran. "The exiled princess leaps like a gazelle across the frozen plain," she told herself.

The windows of the bakery were cheerful squares of gold light, and Nuria stopped to stare at an enormous gingerbread house with chocolate shingles and marzipan pillars. I'd eat the roof first, thought Nuria, even as she found herself whirling suddenly around, answering the warning call of some third eye located in her backbone.

In the air, above the Common, hung Agnes's smoke-face, glowing in the gathering dusk. It stared after Nuria with luminous green eyes. Nuria tried to outstare it, but she turned away first, back to the golden windows. She couldn't help wondering what Agnes might have knitted, and even when she'd wound herself up again and left the Common far behind, she couldn't shake the feeling of that fixed, relentless gaze.

The Smoke-Face

Night had fallen by the time Nuria came to the last rise of the mountain, but she had no trouble keeping to the path. There was more light than there should have been, a faint luminescence that came from the ground and had nothing to do with the waning moon. Is it fox fire? she thought, remembering how decaying wood could shine with an eerie glow. But she had a feeling between her shoulder blades that she was being watched, and she snapped her fingers for Osa to move closer.

The barn was dark, the goat and chickens already asleep, but the cottage was lit from the front where the Avy would be carving his music boxes and clocks. A string of windows shone along the face of the cottage and wound around its sides. There were windows on the inside, too, for the sitting room had been tacked onto an older cottage with windows of its own.

Nuria tried to shrug off the feeling of being watched. She shook herself like a dog and smacked at the door with the heel of her hand. Tawny light spilled over the dusting of snow on the stoop.

"Shake, Osa!" commanded Nuria, for snow sprinkled Osa's back and glinted down her forehead to a widow's peak. How happy the Avy will be! Nuria thought. She couldn't wait to see his face when she told him about his wish. Osa shook, and her eyes shone new-penny copper in the spill of light.

"Nuria Magdelena!" came the Avy's voice, using her given name, which meant she'd better listen. "Close the door before the fire turns to ice. Before I turn to ice, for that matter."

"At once, my sovereign liege!" said Nuria, and kicked the snow off her boots. The cottage smelled wonderfully of stew, and was filled with the ticking of dozens of clocks. Nuria was used to the clocks, but there was one thing she thought she'd never get used to.

"Home," she whispered, looking about her. She'd lived with Aunt Hortense for eight whole years after her parents died, but that had never felt like home.

The Avy sat by a cast-iron stove with short curved silver legs. They made a pair, the Avy and the stove, both short and sturdy and round in the middle, and also shining on top, for the Avy had lost most of his hair. The kitchen was behind the sitting room, visible as a rosy glow through the inside windows, with hanging strings of sausage, ham, and cheese above the trestle table.

"Won't you take off your coat and stay a while?" said the Avy. He always said that when she came through the door. She knew he wanted her to stay, stay forever, but it was still a relief to hear him say it every time she came in.

But she first put out her fists as though she held secrets inside her curled fingers. "I have something to tell you."

Another paper-thin spiral fell to the wood shavings at the Avy's feet. "Sly minx," he said, smiling. "What have you been up to?"

"The families have started to come back! One girl's here already, and she's just my age!"

Nuria counted five long seconds before the Avy moved, and even then he only gestured with his knife as though carving a question mark into the air.

"I knew you'd be happy," she said with deep satisfaction.

"I'm happiest for you," said the Avy, reaching for the big clay jar where they kept their wood. "At last you'll have some friends."

"But I just want one special friend," said Nuria. "Someone to have secrets with. You can't have secrets with a lot of people. Just one girl is all I need to put on the play of *The Snow Queen* for the Revels."

"You and those Revels," said the Avy shaking his head, for Nuria had been determined to put on a play for this festival of dancing, singing, and play-acting that came in January, after Twelfth Night. "But how do you know the children are coming back?"

"Agnes told me," said Nuria, shrugging her coat

onto the broad-timbered floor where it made a small but instant lake of melting snow.

The Avy stared at her coat. "Nuria Magdelena!" he said, just as she'd known he would.

Nuria always threw her coat on the floor and always waited for the Avy's "Nuria Magdelena!" before putting it where it belonged. It was comforting, this routine, every night the same.

She heaved the exasperated sigh she always did and hung the coat on a row of pegs beside her skates. They were brand-new metal skates, her pride and joy. She'd never had anything new before.

"Mine, mine, all mine!" she said in a sing-song chant. "And no one else shall have them."

The Avy beckoned her over to give her a kiss. "No one's going to take them from you," he said. "There's no reason to be such a Grabby Bones anymore."

Nuria draped herself over his back and leaned her cheek against his shoulder, smelling the hickory smoke that lingered in his coarse wool shirt. "Avy!" she said, struck by a sudden thought. "We were talking about your wish to bring the families back! You made the wish this morning, but Agnes's third rule is that you can't talk about it for a month."

The Avy tried to fidget a log into the stove and swore beneath his breath. "I wondered what would happen about that," he said at last. "The way I figure it is this:

if someone already knows you made a wish, you can talk about it with them."

"Do you know what I'd like?" said Nuria, lifting her head and rubbing her cheek. She'd leaned so hard the Avy's shirt had printed tiny dots on her face. "I'd like Aunt Hortense to make a wish for more wishes."

"You don't really mean it!" said the Avy, because that was a terrible fate to hope for anyone. The next person who made a wish for more wishes would replace Agnes as Guardian of the Well, and they'd have to be Guardian until someone else made the same wish. That could be years—decades even!—because every villager knew better than to make that wish, and every villager also knew better than to tell the outside world anything about the magic of the Well.

"I do so mean it!" muttered Nuria, but then to distract the Avy she added quickly, "I have a description for you."

Every time Nuria left the cottage, the Avy said, "Find me a description, if you please." And when Nuria saw what she wanted to describe, she'd find the most beautiful words she could and save them up for him.

"From the mountain," she said, "when you look down on the pond, the leafless trees stand spread against the sky like filigree fans." A feeling like dominoes falling in a row clattered down her spine, and she knew she'd found the right words for the describing game.

"That is beautiful," said the Avy, but now Nuria was the one distracted.

"The northern lights!" she cried, and whirled round to press her face to the window, peering through a spattering of fat snowflakes. She searched the heavens, prepared to be enchanted by luminous streamers and arches of light, but her gaze was finally drawn to the ground where an incandescent head came flowing up the mountain.

She put a palm to the window as though to push it away. "Agnes's knitting," she said. "Why is it coming to the cottage?"

The Avy joined her at the window. "A haunting," he whispered, and for a horrifying moment, Nuria thought he might be afraid. But she must have imagined it, for an instant later, he was the same uncompromising, gravelly Avy.

"Nuria, you're not even *thinking* of making a wish, are you?"

Nuria shook her head fiercely. "Of course not, Avy. Haven't you told me not to, a million times? Anyway, what would I wish for now?"

"Nothing, I hope," said the Avy. "Listen, Nuria. I've told you before how the Well will make a wish go wrong if it can?"

Nuria nodded.

"And also how one wish-gone-wrong often leads to another? It's as though the Well manages to set up rows of bad wishes. It tricks people into making them."

"I know all that," said Nuria. "Why are you telling me?"

"You also know, I think, that usually the Guardian's smoke-things just melt away. But here's something you might not know. Watch out when they don't and begin to follow you! That means you're next in line to make a bad wish."

"But wouldn't that warn you not to make a wish?" said Nuria. "And if the Well's trying to trick you into making a wish, why would it warn you not to at the same time?"

"Maybe because it's too easy to trick people," said the Avy. "Maybe the Well needs more of a challenge, like a very strong horse running with extra weight so it won't win a race too easily. Or maybe it's just to frighten people into doing something foolish. We can never really know.

"Now listen carefully. It's clear, isn't it, that the wish-gone-wrong that made the children vanish made me wish for the families to come back?"

Nuria nodded.

"What if the Well is setting up a chain of bad wishes? Supposing my wish went wrong and is leading you to a bad wish?"

"Because the smoke-thing followed me?"

"Exactly," said the Avy. "Because the smoke-thing followed you."

Nuria felt rather unreal and dreamy, as if she'd been

awakened in the middle of the night to talk about this. "But your wish didn't go wrong. Agnes said Catty Winter's already back."

"The Guardian can never lie," said the Avy slowly. "But you must promise me faithfully to stay away from the Well. I don't want it to trick you into making a wish."

"It can't trick me!" But Nuria promised anyway, spitting on her finger and crossing her heart.

"That's what everyone thinks," said the Avy. "So just see you stay away. Now, is it time for Pidalo Pom?"

In answer, Nuria made fists of her hands and held them in front of her. The Avy did the same, so that his broad, brown hands were squared off against her small, white ones.

Nuria had never told the Avy she knew he could determine who'd win the game of Pidalo Pom. The winner got to choose the song for the singing time they had every night. It was more exciting seeing whether he'd let her win than letting luck make its more capricious decisions.

"Ready?" said the Avy, and he began to recite the names of mountain towns, tapping each of their hands in turn to the rhythm.

> Elyn Glen, Fernway Fen.
> Ab-bey-bur-agh.
> Loch Oldlore, Blackhedge Moor,

Cliffs of Murr-agh.

Pidalo pom. Pidalo pom. Pidalo pidalo pidalo pom.

And on the last "pom," the Avy tapped Nuria's hand.

"I won!" cried Nuria. She paused, pretending to choose a song, but she actually had her choice all ready, since the Avy usually let her win.

"I wonder," she said, "if I'll still get to sing the children's solo on Christmas Eve?"

She'd sung it last year, during the Christmas Eve caroling on the Common, but then, of course, she'd been the only child in town.

"Let's worry about that when the time comes," said the Avy. "Do you have your song?"

"'Darling Johnny,'" she said at last, naming a melancholy song with old-fashioned words she liked to roll around her mouth.

Something still shone too brightly from outside the window, but Nuria turned her back on it boldly, knowing the Avy would protect her if it seeped through some careless crack in the cottage. Nuria had the gift of easy song, and her voice joined the Avy's like a crystal thread, floating high above his.

And it's where have you gone to, my Johnny, my darling?
Where's your spirit gone roaming, my darling, my ain?
They say that the maid from the city's bewitched you:
How I wish you'd return to your own self again!

Later, when Nuria was supposed to be going to sleep, she sat up in bed and looked around her loft. She'd never had a room of her own before, and this was the sweetest, coziest room she'd ever seen. Light from the stove downstairs bounced strange angled shadows off the rafters onto the sloped ceiling. Her bed stood beneath the round window, and a shelf on the opposite wall held a little wooden doll and a music box carved with trailing roses and singing birds.

"My treasures," she whispered. She'd never had anything of her own before she came to live with the Avy. Aunt Hortense had even tried to take away her mother's wedding ring, but Nuria had it back now.

She leaned over the end of her bed to shake the music box. Her coins and the ring jingled together. When she opened the box, the tune of "Darling Johnny" sprang from its pink silk throat. There, everything was still safe. She touched the ring, a circle of tiny garnets set in gold.

"I can't come check on you until you're asleep," the Avy called from downstairs.

"I'm asleep! I'm asleep!" yelled Nuria, and flipped the box closed, making it gulp back its music. She grabbed the doll, Sarah, and fell back into bed.

"Really, I'm asleep," she added, for she could never actually go to sleep until the Avy climbed the ladder to check on her.

The broken spring of the armchair complained as he

stood up, and then the ladder creaked beneath his weight. Nuria squeezed her eyes shut, cradling Sarah in her arm. Sarah was dressed in a scrap of old gingham tied round the middle with a string, for Nuria was not clever with a needle as the Avy was.

Nuria felt the pressure of the Avy's gaze on her face, and barely heavier than that, his hand stroking the hair away from her forehead. Then he was gone, thumping down the ladder, joined by the thump of Osa's tail as she greeted him. The last thing she heard was the familiar sound of the Avy closing the shutters, shutting in the warmth rather than shutting out the light, for both he and Nuria rose with the sun.

At midnight, Osa sprang from her dog's light sleep when a gleaming mass of white poured itself under the cottage door. Osa leapt for it, but it soared far above her head. She hurled herself onto the ladder, snapping and barking and stretching her long wolf's body toward the top.

The Avy rose to check on the commotion, but the gleaming mass was already hidden in the loft, shifting here, stretching there, turning into a smoke-face that watched the sleeping Nuria with burning green eyes. He chided Osa for raising a false alarm, then stroked down her hackles and wondered aloud what she might have been dreaming.

Osa did not lie down again. She growled deep in her throat, and for all the length of that long winter's night paced helplessly at the bottom of the ladder.

Nuria's sleep was troubled. She opened her eyes once, but they were filled with dreams and did not believe what they saw. She closed them again to dream of soldiers crushed by avalanches, of maidens frozen in blocks of ice; and she tumbled restlessly and tugged at the blankets to get warm, because she was chilled to the bone.

The face was gone in the morning. Nuria awoke feeling frightened and, because of that, fierce and cross. Instead of bouncing down the ladder as she usually did, she lay in bed for a moment with Sarah digging into her side. The spiderwebs that laced the angles between the ceiling and its supporting beams were jeweled with little beads of ice that some cold thing had left behind.

Catty

The smell of bacon finally lured Nuria down the ladder. Osa was frantic with delight to see her, rearing onto her back legs and resting her forepaws on Nuria's shoulders. "What a nice kiss!" said Nuria, wiping her face with the sleeve of her nightgown. "How can the Avy say it's disgusting?"

She padded into the kitchen. Steam rose from a big copper pot, whose burnished sides were a rosy reflection of the red-brick fireplace. Nuria leaned into the olive barrel. "I'll go see my new family today."

"Your family?" said the Avy. He grimaced, but that was at the thought of olives for breakfast.

"My family." Nuria felt she owned Catty because she'd thought about her so hard. The olive made her lips pucker, and the smell of brine brought water to her eyes. "Catty will invite me to her house, and we'll swear eternal friendship, and practice the play of *The Snow Queen* for the Revels, and exchange a lock of hair."

"Leave your hair alone, please," said the Avy. "And don't go inviting yourself to her house. Ask her to come here."

"Come here!" Nuria hadn't thought of this before. Invite Catty to the cottage? What if Catty won at Pidalo Pom and got to choose a song for the singing time?

She was shaking her head as the Avy added, "And maybe soon our little school will be full of children."

This was something else she hadn't thought about. She was used to being the only one in school. "Let's not talk about school, not during the Christmas holidays," said Nuria, who liked to pretend she didn't care for her lessons. Then she added darkly, "But I'd better still be first in class."

"Miss Grabby Bones!" said the Avy, as Nuria flung open the shutters.

"I can sled down to the village today!" she said with delight, for the entire mountain was blanketed in snow. It was a soft, spattery snow that caught at the windward sides of trees and sifted into delicate wedges along tree branches.

"Say!" said the Avy suddenly. "Tell me again the name of this new friend?"

"Catty. Catty Winter."

The Avy was silent so long that at last Nuria said, "I can almost hear you thinking."

"I'm just trying to work it out," said the Avy. "Catty Winter was that child, the one child aside from you, who didn't vanish last year."

"What is there to work out?"

"You see," said the Avy, "I wished for the Well to

23

reverse the effect of the wish that took away our children. But if Catty Winter wasn't taken away . . . You see my problem."

"Oh," said Nuria slowly. "But Agnes said that Catty is the first one back, so that means the wish is coming true."

"All the same," said the Avy, "I don't want you going near the Well."

"I already promised about the Well," said Nuria, "but I'll promise again if you want." She spat on her finger and crossed her heart.

"And," began the Avy.

"I know! I know!" shouted Nuria. "And don't forget to wash your face, and don't forget to breathe, and don't forget to milk Salty Lass!" That was their goat, who was as salty as her name. "And don't forget to find a description!" Nuria added this as though it were an afterthought. But it was really the most important of all.

"Yes, indeed," said the Avy gravely. "Find me a description, if you please."

So later, with breakfast eaten and Salty Lass milked and the briefest of washes the Avy would allow, Nuria trotted toward the pond, looking for a description. Her skates hung over her shoulder, flirting with her back at every step, and Osa followed close behind.

She stopped to stare into the huge picture window of the Inn, which had been turned into a holiday village, with tiny wooden houses on sparkling cotton snow.

Nuria recognized the eight miniature reindeer the Avy had carved. She loved those little reindeer. Any other day she would have stood gazing at the tiny Christmas wreaths on the tiny doors, and at the doll-sized holiday skaters on a bright mirror-pond. But Catty was waiting for her, and Nuria tore herself away from the window and turned down Pier Road.

She looked at the houses eagerly, watching for some sign that the other families had also returned. But the windows were all dark and empty, like broken teeth. "I wonder when the other families are going to come," she said, puzzled, as she turned off the road and onto the pier.

The pond today was not bright silver but a great stretch of pewter, which Nuria checked for dangerous dark patches. "All clear," she reported. "But it's the road for you, Miss Osa, the long way round. The crows and I will fly across."

She slipped on her skates and off the pier, waiting for that thrilling moment of merging with the ice. When she'd first skated last year, on curved wooden blades the Avy had carved and strapped to her feet, she had a private fancy that part of her bled through to the ice, and that the ice bled back up to her, so that she and the ice were somehow mingled.

"Wait until Catty sees me!" she cried, trying out her new metal skates, which cut so deep and sharp, so close to the heart of the ice, she almost fell when she tried to stop. But that also meant she could change course just by shifting her balance; and she raced across the ice until she'd almost reached the old Winter place, then started to make fancy swoops and twirls. She looked behind at the lovely tracework she'd left on the ice, a crystalline map of her journey, and she spread her arms like wings and stretched her leg behind her. For just a moment she balanced on one blade, arching her back like the swan-girl she'd once seen in a skating poster. The girl hadn't had such thin red-flannel legs, though.

Maybe Catty would be watching, thought Nuria, looking eagerly at the house, hoping to see a face in one of the windows. But the house had a blind, cut-off look, and it was then she found her description for the Avy. "Cataracts," she murmured, with the familiar thrill of words falling into place. "Windows all draped with cataracts of fine cloth."

Her eyes slid along the downhill slope of the yard to the pond, and a delicious shiver touched her spine. "Something magic is about to happen," she whispered, for she was skating into a fairy-tale scene.

At the edge of the pond stood a sled with filigree runners, the white robes of its driver blending with the blowing snow. It was guarded by a snow wolf, proud, lonely, and still. Nuria skated slowly forward, treating the magic as she would a wild animal, as though any rushed or sudden move might startle it away.

But even that tentative movement was a mistake, for

the magic shivered back, startled, and a moment later it vanished. The fairy-tale filigree faded into commonplace wheels and spokes and other disappointing pieces of equipment Nuria could not name.

Nuria looked at her own nimble feet in their brand-new skates, then at Catty's dark boots resting on a ledge, her heels pushed tidily against the back.

"A wheelchair!" said Nuria.

Catty drew one hand from a white fur muff and beckoned. Nuria's heart leapt with a sort of horrified delight, and she wondered whether Catty could have heard her.

Nuria showed off a little when she reached the shore, jamming her blades sideways to stop with a crystal shower of ice. She looked up smiling from her own clever feet, past Catty's black-stockinged legs and the ermine banding of her coat, which, unlike Nuria's outgrown skirt, respectably covered her knees. But then Nuria's smile faltered because she found herself staring into a flesh-and-blood copy of the smoke-face that, last night, had trailed her up the mountain.

But the smoke-face had been insubstantial and mysterious, and anything less mysterious than the real Catty Winter could not be imagined. She had an ordinary plump face and a scattering of fat freckles high on her cheeks, and her wide, cheerful mouth was smiling.

"Who's your friend?" Nuria waved at the statue of an angel that stood beside Catty. It was the angel's pointy curls that had tricked her into thinking it was a snow wolf.

Catty laughed. "You can really skate, can't you?" She spoke as though she were also saying, "What fun for you!" and her hands danced about like a tangible echo of her cheerful voice.

Nuria stepped onto shore, skates and all. "The Princess Nuria," she said. "Champion skater, at your service." She patted the angel on the head. "Yours, too." The soft snow covered the tops of her boots and sifted down inside. Her feet would soon be wet.

Catty had green eyes, so light a green as to be almost transparent, and they were rimmed with thick, dark lashes.

A book would call them "sooty lashes," thought Nuria. Sooty lashes to match her shiny black princess hair.

"I used to skate until last year," said Catty, her hands dancing away, which made it harder to ignore the lifeless legs below. "I wasn't as plump as I am now, and I could skate to the village in half an hour."

"I can skate there in twenty minutes," said Nuria, even though she'd never tried. Then the meaning of what Catty said caught up with her understanding. "You mean you used to skate!"

"I wasn't always like this. I could walk until last year, when that terrible wish sent away all the children. Then I got very sick, sick as my mother before she died."

"Can you ever get better?"

Catty looked down at her bright button boots, shiny and smooth as though they'd never been worn. "It would take a miracle. That's what the grand doctor in Abbyburgh said. We went there to live so he could make me better, but he can't. He can't work miracles, he says."

"The Avy says most doctors are plaguey fools," said Nuria.

"Plaguey fools," said Catty, and laughed. Nuria laughed too because Catty's laughter was contagious; and they were both still laughing when Catty said, "A wish is a miracle. Will you make a wish for me to walk?"

And then Nuria was the only one still laughing.

"I really mean it," said Catty. "Will you make a wish for me?"

Suddenly Nuria's laughter was gone, and everything was silent.

"We could skate together if you did," added Catty.

"But I'm faster than you, remember?" said Nuria. "Anyway, why don't you make a wish yourself? They're your legs."

Catty's light eyes shifted away from Nuria, and she tucked her hands into her muff. "I used up my wish."

"Used it up!" cried Nuria. "What did you wish for?"

It seemed a long time before Catty answered. "I wished my papa would get married again."

"It didn't work, of course," said Nuria complacently.

"Only the Avy knows how to make a wish. How did your wish go wrong?"

"I must have said my wish so the Well thought it could send me a governess instead of a mother."

"Ooh, a governess," said Nuria. "Is she wicked?"

Catty shook her head and laughed. "Just wait until you see her."

"Oh," said Nuria, disappointed. And then, to console herself, "The Avy's wish came true, anyway. He wished for you to come back—you and the other children." She thought of all those empty houses. "They should be getting here soon."

"So that's what happened," said Catty. "My papa said it was a wish, of course. He's scared to death of wishes, but he was never in one before. He's even more scared now, after those big smoke shapes rushed at us, and there was that pulling-away feeling, and we landed in the parlor with a rather hard bump. But it was worth it; even he thinks so. The first thing he did was blow a kiss to the portrait of my mother. She was the most beautiful child in the village when she was growing up."

Catty smiled as though remembering something pleasant. "But Stuffy was screaming the whole time." Catty made a very funny face with a wide-open screaming mouth.

"Stuffy?" said Nuria.

"Miss D'Estuffier," said Catty. "She's my governess. She loves the city and wants to go back to Abbyburgh."

"Back to Abbyburgh!" cried Nuria. "But you just got here!"

Catty shrugged the heels of her hands into the air. "My papa likes it here best, but we might go anyway because he's so afraid. My mother was in a wheelchair before she died, just like me, and Stuffy's convincing him that it's better in Abbyburgh with doctors, and concerts, and things like that."

"But the city!"

"You look so fierce when you speak," said Catty. "You push your eyebrows way up, like this. Here, this is me, doing Nuria. *But the city!*"

"You should be an actress," said Nuria.

"I want to be an actress," said Catty, suddenly serious. "Except . . ."

"Except what?"

There was a long pause. "Except you have to be beautiful."

"In my show," said Nuria grandly, "there is a rule that no one can be beautiful."

Catty turned her cheek to Nuria as though she were warming it in the sun. "What's your show?"

"It's part of the Revels," began Nuria.

"I was always the star of the Revels," said Catty.

Nuria tried to explain again. "I didn't know how to put on the play of *The Snow Queen* for the Revels, not all alone. But we can put it on together, now that you're here. I'll be Gerda, and you'll be Kai. They're best friends, and Gerda saves him when he gets stolen by the Snow Queen."

Nuria looked Catty over to see what kind of Kai she'd make. Catty was very clean and shiny, and the bit of sailor dress that showed beneath her coat was stiff with starch, and very white. The red ribbons in her hair matched the bow at her collar, and on one of Catty's plump tapering fingers was a little gold ring with a pink enamel rose.

Nuria stared rather hard at this ring. *Miss Grabby Bones,* she finally told herself, then asked aloud, "You don't sing, do you?" She was thinking of the Christmas Eve caroling and how she'd sung the children's solo last year.

"I stopped singing when Miss D'Estuffier told me I don't quite stay on the tune," said Catty. She leaned forward and her strange translucent eyes were bright. "But I'm the actress, so I should be Gerda."

"I'm Gerda," said Nuria.

Catty went on as though Nuria hadn't spoken. "We could use my dress-up clothes for the play."

"But the Avy has a length of silk all set aside to make me a Gerda costume," said Nuria cautiously, because what if using Catty's dress-ups meant that Catty got to be Gerda?

But then she couldn't help asking, "What kind of dress-up clothes?"

"A beaded handbag," said Catty. "Silver shoes."

"Now hear this!" said Nuria. "The Princess Nuria's brilliant new idea. We'll use your dress-ups and have a secret club to put on lots of plays."

"Ooh, a secret club," said Catty.

"We could have a secret handshake, too. Let's twine our fingers together, like this, and tap our thumbs, so." Nuria demonstrated with her own two hands.

"And a secret greeting, too," said Catty. "Something silly like 'Wishing Well.' I know: let's say, 'Well, Well, Wishing Well.'" Catty held out her fingers the way Nuria showed her.

The way Catty said it didn't sound silly at all, but there was nothing for Nuria to do but to take Catty's hand in the secret handshake position. "Well, Well, Wishing Well," they chanted, tapping their thumbs.

This reminded Nuria that Catty wanted her to make a wish on the Well; and in a heartbeat's moment of sudden fright, Nuria wanted to be safely back in the village Square, gazing into the window of the Inn at the cunning little wooden town, nestled into the folds and hills of sparkling cotton snow, and at the eight prancing little reindeer.

Broomarium

There were as many servants living in Catty's house as there were family members. More, if you counted Catty's governess. Wilkes, the manservant, sat in the front hall, fanning himself with his shiny black hat. He was still having palpitations, he said, from yesterday's magical journey to Bishop Mayne. "I should never have carried Miss Catty up that hill to the house just now. It might have been the death of me."

"Ah, you're just a lazy old soul," said his wife, Bertha, whisking off Nuria's coat. Nuria felt funny taking off her coat without hearing the Avy's familiar "Won't you take off your coat and stay a while?" Bertha's black skirts and white apron billowed about her, and even in that small space she looked like a stout ship sailing in a brisk wind.

"It's the dust and damp that's giving me palpitations," she added. Her monstrous white hat bobbled as she opened a tiny, almost invisible door tucked under the curved oak banister. She took a broom from an angular hideaway beneath. "The house has been closed for too long. Now scat, all of you, before you raise any more dust."

The parlor was rather gloomy, with maroon stripes going up and down the walls, and dark-gold stripes going across the chairs, and crimson velvet curtains, which were drawn shut. On the up-and-down stripes hung a portrait of a woman with Catty's light eyes and sooty lashes. *The most beautiful child in the village,* thought Nuria, remembering what Catty had said about her mother.

The Turkish carpet was beautiful, all deep reds and blues, and Nuria tiptoed onto it as though that would keep it from getting dirty. She caught a glimpse of her wild hair in a heavy gold-framed mirror, and she glanced down at her grab-bag mittens and bright red stockings, feeling as mismatched and out of place as she ever had at Aunt Hortense's. A little yellow canary sat in a cage on the parlor table, and Nuria began to wiggle her finger between the bars.

"No fingers, please!" A woman stepped from the shadow of the bay window and tossed a cloth over the cage. Nuria's hand leapt back to her side. "Poor birdie's upset by our trip yesterday."

"At least he didn't scream the way you did," said Catty.

Catty's governess wore black, which, until now, Nuria thought she hated. Aunt Hortense had often worn black; she said it was slimming. But this was quite a different kind of black, glimmering in the firelight with hints of green and blue, and there was probably no one less like Aunt Hortense in the whole world. Nuria couldn't stop looking at the floaty golden hair and the huge blue eyes. A neck like a swan, she told herself.

"We want to play with my dress-ups," said Catty.

"You'll have to tell me where they are," said Miss D'Estuffier. "I knew where everything was in our Abby-burgh house. But here . . ." She encompassed with a sweep of her arm this new house she'd seen only yes-terday for the first time. Her voice was light and laughing, and the very movement of her hand through the air released a smell of sweet violets.

"Papa?" said Catty.

A shadowy sort of man rose from a chair in the cor-ner. Nuria hadn't noticed him before because he'd chosen to sit in the coldest part of the parlor. "I'm so glad you found a friend," said Mr. Winter, nodding at Nuria in a rather melancholy way. "I wonder if I can persuade Wilkes to bring the dress-ups downstairs."

His face didn't quite match up with itself, Nuria realized after a moment, with its youngish pink lips, middle-aged mustache, and oldish thinning hair. She had fun thinking he must have been put together from three different men.

Wilkes brought the dress-ups to Catty's bedroom,

which was on the ground floor, in the library, because it was now too difficult to get her up and down stairs to the real bedrooms.

It's not nearly as nice as my loft, thought Nuria smugly even before she could really see, for the lamp was not yet lit. A great white shape loomed out of the dimness, and she reached out to touch the eyelet draperies of a canopy bed. When Mr. Winter turned up the lamp, dark wood-paneled walls swam into view, and the glass-fronted bookcases glinted. Then he vanished in his shadowy way, leaving the girls alone together.

It took a steamer trunk to hold all Catty's dress-ups. "These could be the Snow Queen's shoes," said Catty, holding up a pair of silver slippers. Nuria reverently picked up a lace shawl and a single lavender glove, but Catty casually rummaged through the frothy, shining pile until she came upon a pink silk dress. "My papa says this goes with my complexion."

Nuria put on a purple taffeta dress, which was far too big for her and all but stood up by itself. "It clashes with your red hair," said Catty.

"Titian, not red," said Nuria, swirling the lace shawl over her shoulders. "My beautiful titian hair!" She spun round and round, loving the whisper of lace and the crackle of taffeta. "I have an idea! Let's sneak into that little broom closet under the stairs. That will be our secret place, and we'll call it—Broomarium!"

"Broomarium!" said Catty. A flush came to her cheeks, and Nuria saw how the pink dress did suit her beautifully. "And you'll be the scout and go on ahead to see whether any of the enemy is around. We can't let them see us."

Nuria put a finger to her lips. "You have to whisper! The enemy has ears as well as eyes." She peered out the door. "All clear!"

The wheelchair was very heavy, and pushing Catty around the door jamb hurt Nuria's wrists. "But valiant spies never complain," she whispered. The taffeta made a terrible rustling as they crept down the hall.

The mops and brooms clattered when Nuria pushed the chair through the tiny doorway. They left the door open a crack, for they had no other light, and she and Catty stared at each other in the not-quite-darkness. Nuria held up a finger for silence. There came the sound of heavy footsteps and a sweeping of skirts, now muffled where they dragged across the carpet, now crisp and almost bright on the floor. "Where can those girls have gotten to?" muttered Bertha.

The air smelled of chocolate when she had passed. "She has cocoa for us," whispered Catty, and they pressed their hands to their mouths to keep in the laughter.

"And now for the mission of our secret club," said Nuria. "We have to make the story of the Snow Queen into a play for the Revels, so listen carefully."

Catty leaned forward, and a slant of light through the door was reflected diagonally in her eyes.

"At the beginning," said Nuria, "a demon's mirror broke, and when the pieces fell to earth a piece got in Kai's heart and another in his eye."

"How did it get in his heart?" said Catty. "Did it go right through his skin?"

Nuria had wondered about this herself. "I think it was magic and melted through." Catty was already caught in the story's enchantment, and Nuria made her voice smooth and rhythmic so as not to break the spell. The almost-dark was just frightening enough to be thrilling as she told Catty how Kai's heart froze solid and everything he saw looked ugly to him. After that he was always mean to Gerda, but she still loved him and was heartbroken when the Snow Queen stole him away.

Nuria had read the story so many times that she'd memorized the part where Gerda finds Kai in the Snow Queen's palace.

"The palace walls were made of the driven snow, and its windows and doors made of the biting winds. And they were lighted by the brightest northern lights."

Nuria made her voice into a spooky whisper. "Immense and cold were the Snow Queen's halls." She swept the shawl from her shoulders, and the white lace billowed like blowing snow, casting a magnified shadow of itself against the wall.

This reminded Nuria of something, and when she

struggled to name it, a fragment of melody came to her. "Lace Dappled Grove," she whispered. It was part of an old song the Avy had taught her.

> My love took me a-walking,
> In the purple dawn;
> Through the lace be-dappled grove,
> By the spotted fawn. . . .

"Why are you moving your lips?" said Catty.

"I'm just remembering the story," said Nuria rather coolly, for she would not share the Avy's songs with anyone. The singing time was her own special thing, and it belonged to her alone.

"Immense and cold," said Catty, reminding Nuria where she'd gotten to.

"And Gerda shed hot tears, which fell upon Kai's chest, and with those tears she melted the ice in his heart." Nuria drew out the end of the story, and to keep the secret, magical feeling alive, she curled her fingers into the secret handshake position.

Catty twined her plump fingers into Nuria's thin ones. "Well, Well, Wishing Well," they chanted. Catty looked up, and again the light slanted through her eyes. "How can I act in the play if I can't walk? That's the thing I want most in the whole world." And there was something about the dark and the warmth of Catty's hand that made Nuria hear the desolation behind Catty's carefree voice.

"We'll get your papa to make a wish," said Nuria.

"He's too afraid," said Catty, and it was this reminder of how cruel the Well could be that made Nuria think of one of its nastiest tricks.

"Oh, Catty! Does Miss D'Estuffier know if you wish for more wishes you get stuck as the new Guardian?"

"No, but we can't warn her about it," said Catty. "The Well's a secret. She didn't believe in magic until yesterday, and now she thinks someone cast a spell. Don't worry. She'll never find out about the Well."

Catty bent closer until Nuria could feel the heat from her cheek. "So you have to make a wish for me, don't you see?"

Nuria drew her hand from Catty's and pressed a finger to Catty's lips. "I can't make a wish. The Avy would never let me. But your papa could. We'll work on him, little by little. That's the way you have to do it with grown-ups. First, we have to find a way to say the wish so it won't go wrong. The Avy will think of something. He knows everything about making wishes. Then your papa can't refuse."

"Maybe not," said Catty doubtfully.

"We'll tie knots in our hair, for luck," said Nuria, demonstrating with her wiry copper hair.

Catty tied a knot in her own sleek, dark hair, then

she grasped Nuria's hand once more. "Well, Well, Wishing Well," they said again, in dark and solemn ceremony.

Later, after Nuria had returned up the mountain and gone to bed, she awoke at midnight filled with thoughts of her new friend. She thought about how Catty fell sick on the very day of last year's awful wish. Nuria didn't believe in coincidence, not where the Wishing Well was concerned, and her eyes opened wide as she thought about this. The fire in the stove below had burned away to nothing, and the night was all a piece of blackness. But then the darkness began to sift into familiar patterns—the tent-shaped space beneath the roof, the curve of snowshoes above the rafters, the bulge of her Sunday dress hanging from a hook.

She shut her eyes, but light began to flow through the thin membrane of their lids, gaining in brilliance and intensity. She opened her eyes again to see what it was, and had to squint for a moment. And then she wished she hadn't, for what she saw was a luminous smoke-sculpture of Catty's face, hanging bodiless before her.

Nuria clutched at her blanket like a baby. Her palm turned the wool damp and clammy, and she tasted saltwater above her lip.

She mustn't tell the Avy. If he knew the face had come again, and that it was Catty's face, he might forbid her to see Catty, and that would be unbearable.

Gradually the smoke-face dimmed and began to disintegrate. Like someone rotting, thought Nuria, wishing she'd never read a single ghost story. She waited until it had faded into nothing, then pulled the blanket over her head.

"I mustn't tell him," she said to herself. "I mustn't tell the Avy."

The Wishing Words

It was almost as much fun sneaking things into Broomarium as it was playing there. The first day they sneaked a candle through enemy territory, for they'd need light when they began to turn the story of the Snow Queen into a play. The candlestick was hung about with crystal prisms, which glittered beautifully when the candle was lit.

The next day they brought three sparkling necklaces that had belonged to Catty's mother. The girls pretended they were real diamonds and not just made from paste. "It's best to keep your precious gems in a very secret spot," explained Nuria. They hung them on the wall to shimmer in the candlelight.

"They don't look like paste," said Nuria. "My mother's ring has real garnets, and they don't sparkle like that."

Then Bertha gave them a tin of cookies, and from the dining room sideboard they took two flowered china cups, thin and translucent as eggshells. "These are our provisions," said Nuria, shaking the cookie tin. "And we can pour sugar and water into the teacups and pretend it's tea."

By the fourth day, Broomarium was splendid. Nuria hung the lace shawl on some hooks meant to hold dustpans and dusters, and it cast a magnified pattern of itself on the wall behind.

Nuria tried not to think about the smoke-face, which had awakened her every night since she'd met Catty. That was the only shadow on her happiness. She had the Avy in the cottage up the mountain, and she had a friend in a secret hideaway; and these pieces of her life fit together like the pieces of a puzzle, finished at last.

"Lace Dappled Grove," she whispered, invoking her secret name for their secret place, as though that would exorcise her memory of the smoke-face. "Lace Dappled Grove."

"There you go, moving your lips again," said Catty. She imitated Nuria, opening the round O of her mouth like a fish.

The heat rose in Nuria's cheeks. "It's rude to imitate!" she said. "And I'll never tell you the secret thing I was thinking. It's something private, with the Avy."

"I don't imitate," said Catty. "I act! I'm the actress, so that's why I should have the big part in the play and be Gerda."

"The play is my idea," cried Nuria, "and Gerda's part

is my part, so don't think you will do it! And the Avy's making me a Gerda costume all of apricot silk, which won't fit you!"

They sat looking at each other, both trembling with rage, while the mops and brooms cast thin-waisted shadows across their cheeks and hair.

Bertha's familiar footsteps came near, accompanied by the familiar play of her skirts on the carpet, then on the floor, and as she passed Broomarium, she said quite distinctly, "Where can those teacups have gotten to? Seems like the fairies have been at work again."

They did not laugh, but this broke the tension, and Catty finally said fretfully, "And you haven't asked your Avy about how to say the wish for me to walk again."

At least she hadn't asked Nuria to make the wish, and Nuria felt a warm rush of relief, which made her expansive and generous. "Tonight," she said. "I'll ask him tonight."

But she did not ask him that night. She was too busy worrying about the smoke-face and steeling herself for its midnight appearance. She'd seen it four times now; and regular as the Avy's clocks, it would come again tonight.

The whole year past, since she'd lived with the Avy, she'd fallen asleep as soon as the Avy came to check on her. But now, if she slept at all, it was only for a few minutes at a time, and she always woke just before midnight. Her inner clock had set itself to march along with the ticking of the real clocks, and she was glad, for it gave her a chance to sit up and press her back into the pillow. She hated the thought of being caught asleep, the bony beads of her spinal column turned out toward the smoke-face.

The mass of smoke slipped into the loft just as the clocks announced midnight. It flowed to its spot above Nuria's bed, already swimming into focus as Catty's face.

Nuria was suspended inside her own body, suspended as the smoke-face was suspended before her; and she and the smoke-face were two stillnesses inside a room of ticking clocks and passing time. It wasn't until the smoke-face grew fuzzy around the edges that Nuria's blood began to wheel once more through her body. It made a roaring in her ears, and she struggled not to cry out for the Avy. He'd never let her play with Catty again if he knew. But some inside part of her was screaming, and she pushed through a tangled web of dreams to find the Avy standing at her bedside.

The Avy set his candle on the floor, and the shadows leaped onto her coverlet. The thin-lipped moon did nothing to drive them away. "Did I scream again?" said Nuria. Her hair was plastered to her head with sweat.

"This makes the fifth night," said the Avy. He brushed her hair back from her forehead, then rubbed at her fingers, which were white and tense around her doll.

"My heavens, child. You're cold as ice!" He lifted the candle to Nuria's face. Her pupils shrank back against the light.

"Avy," she said slowly, "Catty and I are playing a new game we call Wishing Well, and we're trying to make wishes that the Well would really grant—ones that wouldn't go wrong, I mean. Of course, Catty wishes to be able to walk. How would you say that wish?"

"First," said the Avy, "before another second goes by, I want your solemn promise that this is only a game and that she's not really going to make a wish."

"May my body be roasted over hot coals," said Nuria, spitting on her finger and crossing her heart.

"Oh," said the Avy, looking surprised, as though he'd expected more of a fight. But it was all right to make the promise. It was Catty's papa, not Catty, who was to make the wish.

"Nuria, you have the foolish notion I know how to wish on the Wishing Well. But if I do, where are the rest of the families? And I can't even guess why the Well is starting to freeze."

"Starting to freeze?" said Nuria, startled.

"It's happened only a few times in my memory, and none of us knows why. At the last council meeting . . ."

"Avy!" said Nuria, because he was beginning to mutter grown-up talk to himself. "Catty's not going to make a wish!"

The Avy sighed. "Tell me again what she wants?"

"To be like me," said Nuria. "To have legs like mine, to run and skate like me."

"You might think of wishing that Catty had a body like yours. Something along those lines."

I wish, thought Nuria, rehearsing it silently, that Catty had a body just like mine. The Avy was looking at her in a funny way, and she pressed her mouth into a line in case she'd been moving her lips.

"There's something you're not telling me," said the Avy, beckoning with his finger as though he could lure words of confession from her mouth.

"Have I thanked you yet for making me that beautiful Gerda costume?" said Nuria. "O distinguished patriarch. . . ." Her jaw pushed itself open in a yawn.

The Avy laid a finger on her lips. "Your eyes are closing. Shall we sing you to sleep?"

Nuria opened her eyes so wide they prickled with tears. "I'm not tired!" She patted his hand. "But we could sing for you, poor sleepy dear."

"Only three days till Christmas," said the Avy. "It's time we left out food for the Christ Child. Almonds and oranges . . ."

"Honey and sugar-cream," continued Nuria. "That's the 'Giving Song.' Shall we Pidalo Pom for who gets to begin?"

"I'm too tired," said the Avy. "The honor is yours."

Nuria sang out the question.

> What shall we give to the son of the Mother?
> What shall we give to the infant so mild?

The Avy sang back the answer.

> Almonds and tangerines, honey and sugar-cream.
> Apricots, oranges, mint growing wild.

The Avy cupped his hand around the candle flame. "Sleep, Nuria. Sleep." And under the power of this suggestion, Nuria's eyelids fluttered closed, shutting her back into sleep where she dreamed the Well had turned to ice. She pushed at its thick, translucent walls, working through the ice with her own warm hand to snatch at the shadows of flying birds.

Nuria didn't go straight to Catty's house the next morning. She went to the Well instead. Maybe Agnes could tell her about the haunting. She'd thought this through countless times and couldn't understand why the smoke-face came to her each night. The Avy said a smoke-thing came to someone who was going to be caught in the Well's game of making one bad wish lead to another. But that meant the Avy's wish went wrong, which couldn't be, for Catty had come back.

Nuria walked carefully, delicately, through the

deserted streets that morning, for at breakfast, the Avy
had said her skin was waxy and her eyes were hollow.
She hadn't been able to see this herself because they
had no mirror, only the big copper pot, which stretched
and twisted her reflection into a girl she didn't recog-
nize. But Nuria liked the Avy's description, and she
practiced looking romantic and frail.

"A coin for passage to your heart's desire. That is the
first rule."

For the first time in Nuria's memory, the Well was
covered with a sheet of ice. She heard the Avy's words
from last night, which seemed now like a dream: "And
I can't even guess why the Well is starting to freeze."

It was too slippery to fling herself upon the rim, so
she curled the fingers of each hand inside minute
crevices, pressing so hard her fingers turned white. She
crammed her toes between the rocks, and this gave her
the purchase she needed to spring up the granite wall.
She couldn't wait to see the hummingbirds' eggs.

But there was nothing left of spring. Sprays of ice
winked up at Nuria, dripping and draping from rose to
rose and looping about the nest. Some winter fairy
might have trailed a careless wand, spinning fragile,
deadly bridges through the air.

"One wish each lifetime; one cycle of the moon to
repent and call it back. That is the second rule."

Nuria did not scream, but everything became at

once more distant and distinct as she whispered, "Agnes! What happened?"

"And for that cycle of the moon, your lips are locked in this: To no one may you speak of your wish. To no one but to me, for your wish is my wish too. That is the third rule."

The hummingbirds were hovering frantically over their nest, and Nuria saw with horror that they were too tiny to melt the frosty cocoon that laced the eggs. The nightingale perched motionless on a sugar-spun branch, her head tucked in the insulated pocket under her wing. As for the roses, they glistened with tiny ice diamonds that sparkled deep inside their hearts and fanned along the whorled edges of their petals.

"Just a little tantrum," said Agnes. "The Well had its next wish set up so nicely. It can get frustrated, too."

Nuria's head jerked up, and she slid to the ground to face Agnes. Agnes was smiling the kind of smile that was mostly inside her mouth and barely reached her lips.

"I hope the Well doesn't get its wish," said Nuria loudly. "Greedy thing. It can't make someone wish for something the person doesn't want."

"Quite right," said Agnes. "But what if the person does want?"

These words chilled Nuria quite as much as the sight of the frozen Well, but she ignored the cold finger that ran down her spine and spoke up boldly. "Why did you send that smoke-face off to haunt me? The Avy's wish didn't go wrong."

"Shall I knit you up an answer?" said Agnes. "A smoky green should go nicely with that red hair."

"Titian!" said Nuria, automatically. But then she stepped back, away from Agnes, and with a mumbled excuse, she turned and ran off, running more quickly than a frail storybook heroine would ever run, and she didn't look back to see what Agnes might be knitting.

But she remembered about her frail, heroic self before she got to Catty's, and by the time she arrived, she'd convinced herself she was an outcast princess, struggling through the snow. She went straight to the parlor mirror to examine her face of royal suffering.

"What on earth are you doing?" said Catty, who was sitting near the fire, taking impossibly small stitches in a stretch of white fabric.

"Do you think I look ill?" asked Nuria, peering at her reflection above the mantle. The Avy was right. Her skin was pale and had begun to take on the faint lustrous sheen of a candle. She stared at the dark smudges beneath her eyes and felt a dull ache spread through her skull.

Mr. Winter's face appeared in the mirror over her shoulder, and they smiled looking-glass smiles at each other. "Mirror, mirror on the wall," said Mr. Winter, "who's the fairest one of all?" The top of Miss

D'Estuffier's head stepped into this reflected world, curving above Mr. Winter's shoulder.

"That would have to be Catty's mother," said Nuria at last.

"The most beautiful child in the village," said Catty rather mournfully.

"But remember," said Nuria, "no one who's beautiful gets to be in my play."

There was a long pause, as Nuria looked first at the curve of Miss D'Estuffier's bright hair, then at the reflection of the portrait on the opposite wall.

"Isn't that lucky for you, Catty!" said Miss D'Estuffier in her sweet voice. "I know you'll make a magnificent Gerda."

"Gerda!" Nuria cried out. "That's my part. Catty's not playing Gerda!"

"You said you wouldn't tell!" said Catty, jabbing her sewing hand at Miss D'Estuffier, piercing the air with her needle.

Miss D'Estuffier put her fingers to her mouth. "It slipped my mind, dear," she said. "So sorry."

Nuria rushed at Catty's wheelchair and swung it toward the parlor door, brushing past Miss D'Estuffier. "Move aside, varlet," she muttered. She was dimly aware of Mr. Winter gazing after her in astonishment, but Miss D'Estuffier stood quite still, a faint smile on her face. Nuria pushed Catty off the carpet, onto the hallway floor, and through the door into Broomarium.

"You sneak," she hissed, not daring to raise her voice for fear of the grown-ups' listening ears. "You snake!" She liked hissing, too; it made her think of serpents and venom.

"I don't see why you're making a fuss," said Catty, her fingers flying into the air in delicate surprise. "I told you I wanted to be Gerda, and you said you wanted to be Gerda."

"Miss Grabby Bones!" said Nuria, turning the Avy's description of her own self against Catty. "And you told them not to say anything!" That was the worst, really: Catty sneaking off to tell the grown-ups she was going to be Gerda, as if telling them would make sure it happened.

"I was going to invite you to the cottage tomorrow night," said Nuria, inventing this on the spot. She'd make Catty sorry. "The Avy and I will put out our gifts for the Christ Child. Honey and nuts and cream. But you can't come now."

"I wouldn't come if you begged me on bended knees!" said Catty.

It was dim in Broomarium, for the candle was unlit, and the jewels hanging on the walls looked dreary and false. "Paste," said Nuria. "It's all paste."

"My mother's jewels," said Catty. "I'll take them back, and you can never come here again."

Nothing could be worse than this. Their own secret place, closed forever. "You can take your mother's jewels," said Nuria, feeling more hateful than she'd felt since she'd left Aunt Hortense's. "But you'll never be beautiful the way she was."

Catty was silent, and Nuria pushed the door open a crack to see her better. Catty's face was caught in a trickle of grayish light. She'd closed her eyes, and Nuria smiled a thin-lipped smile. Victory for Nuria the Magnificent!

But then a tear welled up in the corner of Catty's closed eye, and then another, until under Nuria's horrified gaze, they began to pour down Catty's face.

Catty actually looked very pretty like that, her head tilted back, great tears leaking from under the upward curl of her long lashes.

This was a new feeling for Nuria, to have such power she could make a person cry. She shifted from foot to foot, then put out her hand awkwardly. "It wasn't true, what I said just now."

"Yes, it was," said Catty.

"No, it wasn't," said Nuria. "I promise you." And although Catty couldn't see her, she spat on her finger and crossed her heart. "I can tell you something that will make you happy."

Catty swallowed hard. "I'll never be happy again."

"But the Avy told me the words your papa should

say to the Well. *I wish Catty had a body just like Nuria's.*"

"He'll never do it," said Catty. But she had opened her eyes and was wiping her cheek with the back of her hand.

"We'll make him say it," said Nuria, willing to say almost anything to keep Catty as her friend. Nuria had the Avy, but she couldn't play with him the way she did with Catty. You couldn't have secrets and lace-dappled hideaways with a grown-up. Nuria couldn't bear to lose any of that.

"You'll love putting out the honey and nuts and cream for the Christ Child," she added, because now she had to turn her threat into a promise and invite Catty to the cottage. The Avy sometimes said she'd regret words spoken in anger. He'd been right about that, for once, although she'd never tell him so.

"Tell me those wishing words again?" said Catty.

"A body just like Nuria's. I wish Catty had a body just like Nuria's."

Words of Anger

Nuria waited until breakfast to tell the Avy about inviting Catty to the cottage. Maybe he'll say no, she thought, trying to look as sick as possible, which wasn't hard. She felt horribly dragged out after last night. This made the sixth time she'd seen the smoke-face. It was just as well Catty was going visiting with her papa and that Nuria couldn't play with her today, for Nuria's eyes were full of sand, her brain bouncing against her skull like a rubber ball.

But the Avy merely nodded and stirred his coffee slowly as he thought it over.

"If Catty's to come tonight," he said, studying Nuria over the red-and-white oilcloth, "you must promise to stay at home this morning and sleep."

"Sleep!" said Nuria. "It's broad daylight!" She glared at the Avy as though he'd ordered up this sturdy sun that glanced off the snow into the cottage. "How do you expect an ordinary mortal like me to sleep with all these clocks ticking?"

"Oh, I wouldn't call you an ordinary mortal," said

the Avy. "But these nightmares of yours do worry me, and you're pale as a ghost."

Nuria swung around to look in the copper pot. Her distorted face peered back at her, unsubstantial and wavery, as though she were filled with mist instead of solid bone and good red blood.

"Can't we ever get a mirror?" she said. "When I'm sixteen and have to put up my hair, it'll come out all lumpy."

"We'll talk about it when you're sixteen," said the Avy. "But it won't be worth looking into if you don't get some rest now."

Nuria's fingers crept over the table toward last night's leftover cake. "Nuria's tired and needs some cake, poor orphaned child."

The Avy's hand darted out and pulled the plate toward him. He could move astonishingly quick when he wanted. "Hands off!" he said, but he sounded sad instead of scolding. "I suppose someday you'll learn you don't need to grab for everything anymore."

"But the mice will get it," said Nuria. "They just love that lemon-hazelnut icing."

"The only mouse around here is you, Miss Grabby Bones."

Nuria sighed and lay down, rolling her back along the bench. If she adjusted her eyes just right, she could make the ceiling look like the floor and pretend she was walking on it. How funny to have a lamp sticking out of the floor.

"But when Catty comes," she said, "I don't want to sing. Not with her here."

"Not sing!" said the Avy, astonished. "But we have to sing the 'Giving Song' when we put out our gifts."

"I just don't want to," she said. "Our songs are special, just between you and me. Like the describing game."

"Nuria! Singing isn't something you use up, like a piece of cake. There's plenty to go around."

"You don't understand," she said, turning her head to look at him under the table. But he was standing up, the right angle of his knees disappearing as she watched. He couldn't see her, so she stuck out her tongue. She'd never make him understand—understand what? She barely knew herself. Just that the Avy was the only one who'd ever loved her, and she didn't want to share the special things she had with him, not even with Catty.

"I'm going to the village to see if any of the other families has arrived," said the Avy. "I'll ask Mr. Winter if Catty can come for dinner."

"I'll tie a knot in my hair for luck," said Nuria without enthusiasm.

"It seems to me you have enough knots in your hair," said the Avy. "And don't forget to milk Salty Lass. We'll need cream for our gifts to the Christ Child tonight."

"I never forget!" yelled Nuria. The force of her voice made her head vibrate on the bench.

The Avy put his fingers to his ears. "Nuria, you'll shatter the stove with that voice. You've already shattered me. Meet me at the Common at sunset, and I expect to see you looking rested. Oh, and find me a description, if you please."

Now here was something for Nuria to do, something solid and satisfying. She'd go skating and look for a description, and leave even the memory of her midnight phantom behind. But first she'd curl up on the sitting-room armchair and close her eyes, just for a few minutes. That way, if the Avy asked, she could truthfully say she'd rested.

Nuria sat up three hours later. "Plagues take it!" she cried, borrowing a favorite expression of the Avy's. The whole morning was gone; sleeping was such a waste of time. She stuffed a slice of bread into her coat pocket and sledded to the village. Her footsteps clicked down the awful quiet of Pier Road, the ghost houses looking even more desolate and shabby in the bright sun. A loose shutter banged in a little gust of wind. She heard herself gasp and then, as though she were standing outside herself, heard the sound of her own feet pounding down the road and onto the pier.

"A description," she said as she strapped on her skates. "A description for the Avy!"

She eased onto the ice and cast her words in front of her, threading the air with her voice and tugging it taut with a bright invisible line. And the ice flowed into her legs—or maybe it was that her legs flowed into the ice—and even when she took to the air in a jump there was some secret that whispered between the ice and her feet.

She began with baby jumps but grew confident by the end of the afternoon. Her feet, from habit now, had taken her near the old Winter place. "I wish the Avy could see me do this!" she said, leaping into the air. She landed on her backside, then bowed to the angel statue watching from the shore. "Please restrain your applause."

A thin winter sunset unrolled behind the black-lace treetops, and she searched for the right describing words. "Lavender gauze," she said finally. "Lavender gauze mixed with a spoonful of light." She stood up and brushed the snow from her skirt. It was time to meet the Avy; maybe she could beat him to the Common.

But the Avy was already waiting. Nuria sneaked up behind him. "Boo!" She could at least pretend she'd gotten there first.

She'd never succeeded in taking him by surprise, and this time was no different. "Look at that ice, will you," he said, without turning around. "It's spreading."

Nuria followed the direction of his pointing finger.

The ice was thicker than yesterday, beginning to spill outside the Well in wind-blown courses that glistened in the lavender half-light. "Agnes said the Well is having a tantrum," she said, remembering Agnes's little inside smile.

The Avy wheeled around in one of his surprising, snake-quick moves. "The Well is not a plaything, Nuria! Didn't you promise me you'd stay away from it?"

"I wasn't playing!" said Nuria indignantly, because she hadn't broken her promise just by talking to Agnes. "I had to ask Agnes something."

"Nuria Magdelena!" said the Avy. "It comes to the same thing."

"Nuria Magdelena to you!" said Nuria furiously. "Do you think I'd break my promise! I'm not going to tell you about my lavender-gauze sunset."

"If you think that's not breaking your promise," said the Avy, "then I release you from it altogether, since it clearly means nothing to you."

"You're just like Aunt Hortense," said Nuria. Her lips were white with rage at this injustice. "Always disappointed in me." There was no truth to this, and she knew it; but if the Avy could be unfair, so could she.

"Have a care for what you say, Miss Nuria," said the Avy. "Your tongue will get you into trouble one of these days."

They did not speak another word until Mr. Winter's

carriage rumbled into the Square. Nuria didn't like the tender way the Avy wrapped Catty in a pile of blankets and packed her onto the sled like a china ornament. The sight of Miss D'Estuffier's floaty golden hair and huge blue eyes didn't give her the usual bell-ringing feeling inside; and she didn't even bother to brush accidently-on-purpose against Miss D'Estuffier's white fur cape.

They started up the mountain in silence, until Nuria could bear it no longer and tugged at the Avy's sleeve. "Avy," she said, "O judge of sage advice."

"What is it now?" His voice was back to normal, all rumble and gravel; in fact, he might be trying not to laugh.

"Catty wants to be Gerda in our play, but she was supposed to be Kai."

"You mean you decided I was supposed to be Kai," began Catty, but Nuria interrupted.

"You see how it is!" said Nuria. "And I told her you've already started the Gerda costume for me."

"What if you make Kai's part just as exciting?" said the Avy. "Then it might be easier to give up Gerda's part."

"Oh, Avy!" said Nuria in a disgusted voice, but the Avy held up a finger.

"Hush! There's no moon, and the path gets tricky here."

"There's not *no* moon," said Nuria. But this was just

for the sake of argument, for the moon was no more than a luminous sliver, curling above the shrugging shoulder of the earth.

"Hush!" The Avy steered them past the difficult bit. "And now," he said, "let's hear about that lavender-gauze sunset."

"Not now, Avy!" Nuria whisper-hissed. "Remember what I told you this morning? About the songs and the describing game?"

"Foolishness!" said the Avy, but Nuria clamped her lips together, and they ended the climb as they had begun, in silence.

Nuria had already laid her treasures on the kitchen table for Catty to see: her music box, her skates, and her doll. Beside them the Avy had set out the gifts for the Christ Child. There were almonds, tangerines, honey, cream in a bowl, and sugar in a cone of paper. Catty sat in the sitting-room armchair, which the Avy had dragged to the kitchen fire.

"What a lot of ticking," said Catty, squirming about and making the springs creak.

"Grumble, grumble yourself!" said Nuria to the chair.

The Avy handed Catty the cream and sugar, and a whisk. "Tell me if you're sitting on the broken spring. Nuria, wrap that shawl around Catty, will you? And Nuria, won't you take off your coat and stay a while?"

Nuria just folded her arms across her chest and

glared at him. That's what he always said when she came in. How dare he use his special I-want-you-to-stay words in front of Catty!

The Avy shrugged. "Have it your own way."

"You can have your own way about something else, too," said Catty. "You get to be Gerda in the Revels. I won't be here because we're going back to Abbyburgh right after Christmas."

"Going back!" said Nuria, feeling a strong hand grip her heart and wring out all its juices. Stuffy had won. "Why didn't you tell me?" She set the music box on the table and flipped it open.

"I tried to tell you going up the mountain," said Catty. "But you interrupted."

The mechanical soul of the music box could not do justice to the melancholy sweep of the song, but despite that, tears began to rise through the hot springs behind Nuria's cheeks. She thought of the days and weeks and months ahead without Catty and stared at the oilcloth as though the sight of it might repel unwanted tears.

"I wish I could skate again," said Catty, reaching for Nuria's skates. Her thumb left a ghostly shadow on one silver blade. She stirred her finger in the music box, making the coins and the ring jingle together. "Your mother's ring." She put it to her lips as though she were sucking some secret meaning from it, then slipped it on her finger. "I don't have a ring from my mother."

Nuria swallowed the lump of tears where she felt it melt into her heart, waiting to escape again at some new grief. "We have to get your papa to make the wish," she whispered. "We just have to."

Catty shook her head. "I know he never will. He's too afraid."

This was the most unfair thing that had happened. Nuria could actually taste bitterness rising from her throat, and underneath there was a hot stream of resentment against the Avy.

"Does your papa like to play games?" she said, grasping at straws. "Would he play Pidalo Pom to decide whether he'd do it?" But even that, she thought, would be a bold move for pale, melancholy Mr. Winter.

"Pidalo Pom?"

"You use it to choose things," said Nuria. "We could play Pidalo Pom to see who gets the leftover cake. It has lemon-hazelnut icing."

"No cake before dinner," said the Avy.

"You don't have to tell me!" said Nuria impatiently. "But we can play Pidalo Pom for it now." She sat backward on the bench, facing Catty, and held out her fists. It was very warm there, near the fire, for she still hadn't taken off her coat.

"I don't know if I like hazelnut," remarked Catty, but she'd already followed Nuria's example of balling her hands into fists, and she held them out to Nuria.

The Avy drew a stool to the girls, and then there were three of them, three sets of fists in a circle, asking like begging dog paws for a piece of cake.

Elyn Glen, Fernway Fen.
Ab-bey-bur-agh.

Nuria decided to forgive the Avy when he let her have the cake. She knew he would. That would be his way of apologizing; and she'd fling her arms around his neck and whisper that they'd never leave each other.

Loch Oldlore, Blackhedge Moor,
Cliffs of Murr-agh.
Pidalo pom. Pidalo pom. Pidalo pidalo pidalo pom.

The Avy tapped Catty's hand.

"Catty won," said Nuria slowly. She could not even look at the Avy. He had chosen Catty over her, and only the brightness of her eyes betrayed her fury.

"I need to tell Catty a secret," she said coldly to the Avy. "Will you kindly step away?"

The Avy raised his eyebrows. "Since you ask so nicely."

Nuria stared at him without blinking until he turned away, then she cupped her hands around Catty's ear.

"I want you to stay and be my very best friend. I'll

wish for some legs for you. I'll do it, I will." There, that would show the Avy.

Catty was sliding the garnet ring up and down her finger. Next to it she wore her own ring, with the pink enamel rose. "When will you do it?"

"Tomorrow," said Nuria. "But don't worry about pledging eternal gratitude or anything."

"Do you swear to do it?" said Catty. "Prick your finger and swear on blood!"

Nuria looked at her fingertip, closed up so neatly without a single seam. "You'll never get me to prick my finger."

"This all sounds rather sinister," said the Avy, looking from one girl to the other, only half smiling.

"Not sinister at all," said Nuria lightly to hide her fear that the Avy might be right.

Catty just smiled. There was an expression Nuria had once heard, something about a cat with cream. She understood it now as she looked at Catty, secret and veiled as a cat, but purring beneath at the prospect of cream. And suddenly Nuria felt very cold, although she was still sitting near the fire, and she still hadn't taken off her coat.

The Wish

"This is highly irregular," said Agnes.

"Does that mean you won't do it?" said Nuria, trying not to sound too hopeful. "Or that you can't?" Her headache was back, her brain corrugated and seamed as a walnut, pressed between the two halves of her skull.

"She'll have to do it," said Catty. "It's her obligation."

"It is," said Agnes in what seemed to be agreement, but there was a wary rise to her voice that suggested a question rather than a comment. Nuria glanced from Agnes to the Pillar as though, from long association with Agnes, it might know the true meaning of her statement. But the Pillar just looked back at Nuria with its hollow, stony eyes, and she finally turned away.

The sun on this Christmas Eve day was a mottled smear that hung in the sky like a bruise. Nuria's thoughts took odd turns, getting lost in dark passages and corners, and her mouth tasted sour as though she were a mirror of this jaundiced, brooding afternoon.

"We shall have to alter the rules for this wish," said Agnes.

Nuria pressed an index finger to each temple. Maybe she could feel her brain pounding through the fragile tissue of skin.

"A wish made by one person for another must run by different laws than a wish made on behalf of the wisher alone." Agnes folded her hands in her lap and muttered a bit.

"*A coin for passage* . . . Yes, one coin will do well enough. There is only one wish after all." She looked at the Well, then nodded, as though it had sent her some secret message. "*One cycle of the moon* . . . Ah, here we come to it."

Agnes raised her eyes and spoke directly to Nuria. "Should you repent of this wish and want to take it back, both you and Catty will have to revoke it together. It is, after all, a wish that involves the two of you."

"Oh, we'll never take it back," promised Catty, reminding Nuria of her own boast to Agnes just last week. *I'd be careful how I said it,* she had said, pointing to the Pillar. *I wouldn't need to take it back, not like him.* Nuria looked at the Pillar now, and it met her gaze with the same secret, stony face.

Agnes shrugged. "Many have said the same. Now show me your coin."

Nuria wrapped her fingers around the three cold

71

metal discs in her pocket. "Does it hurt to make a wish?"

"That depends on the wish," said Agnes.

"Vastly comforting," said Nuria, opening her hand. "And here, ladies and gentlemen, we have a choice of copper, nickel, and silver."

"Silver perhaps," said Agnes. But she seemed to be looking past the coins, not at them, as though she might be reading another fortune in Nuria's palm, following her lifeline and finding it short.

Nuria closed her fingers and raised the coin to toss it in. She had no desire to watch the coin fall, no stomach to see the birds suspended between life and death, the roses encased in their tissue of ice. And the hummingbirds' eggs . . .

Nuria couldn't bear to think of those eggs.

She looked behind her to record the scene on her memory, painting a picture of the day she made her wish. Catty sat on the sled behind Nuria, and Osa lay by the Pillar, licking her paws, trying to melt bits of sharp, granular snow lodged between the pads.

Nuria opened her fingers and let the coin fall.

Everything was frozen and still. Nuria waited for the sound of metal striking water. It was so quiet she half expected to hear the heartbeat of a hummingbird.

"Agnes has it!" said Catty sharply.

"It has not been found acceptable," said Agnes, holding the coin between her thumb and forefinger and pecking it through the air in a silent message for Nuria to take it back.

Nuria slipped it inside her mitten, warming it up between the caress of wool and flesh. She was secretly happy that the Well had more commonplace tastes than she had supposed and wondered whether she should offer her nickel piece when a copper one might do just as well. But she'd already offered both coins and didn't dare back out now. She held out the nickel.

"I think not," said Agnes. "I see now. It must be Catty who gives the coin."

"Give me one of them," said Catty, reaching toward Nuria and waving her closer. Her talkative hands had been very quiet all day. "I didn't bring anything with me."

"You must have brought it," said Agnes. "It need not be yours, but it must be precious to you."

"But I don't have anything," began Catty, patting at her pockets to show they were empty. But then her expression changed, or rather her expression vanished, leaving her stony and secret as the Pillar.

"I did bring something," she said, "just in case we might need it."

She thrust out a hand crossed with gold, and Nuria had to step forward to see what it was. There, on Catty's palm, lay a row of garnets set in gold.

"My mother's ring!" said Nuria. "I don't want to throw it in the Well. Here, give it back."

Catty closed her fingers round the ring. "I didn't take it to throw in the Well," she said. "I would never do that. I thought of hanging it next to my mother's jewels in Broomarium because it's our secret treasure place."

"But it's not made of paste," said Nuria, who was secretly rather cross she hadn't thought of this herself. "The Lord High Chancellor will take it under advisement. What else do you have in your pockets?"

But it was on her finger that Catty finally found the coin. Both she and Nuria saw it in the same instant. "Your pink rose ring," said Nuria.

"But my papa gave it to me," said Catty.

"That's a whining voice, the Avy would say," said Nuria.

Catty looked at the ring for a long time, then drew it off her finger.

When Nuria tossed this new coin into the Well, she waited only a moment before her listening ear heard it greet the water with a faint sigh.

"It has been found acceptable," said Agnes. "You may make your wish."

Now that the moment had arrived, Nuria found her walnut brain could not produce the wishing words that had come so easily to her in earlier careless days. But everyone was waiting for her. Agnes was waiting, Catty was waiting. The Well was waiting, too. It had already eaten Catty's ring and was very likely growing hungry for its second course.

"I wish," said Nuria, licking her lips, which froze and cracked in the cold air. She wiped her mouth on her sleeve, but that only made it worse. "I wish," she said again, "that Catty had a body just like mine!"

She heard her voice turn high and strange. At the same moment, a sudden mist dropped from nowhere and swirled about her as though it were being stirred with a spoon. It thickened with each rotation into a cloud that reminded Nuria of a gigantic marble, all swirls of gray and copper with a twist of gold at the eye. Nuria found herself standing in the eye of the marble, skewered by its hot gold stare. After a moment, she felt an insistent tug, then a sudden *whoosh!* that sucked her painlessly away.

She thought that she was floating off from her body, and even as this impression formed, the gold eye began to dim and draw in on itself. As that happened, Nuria's headache disappeared so completely that only its absence reminded her of its former presence. She'd all but forgotten about her pounding walnut brain. Her legs turned numb, and she grimaced, thinking of the pins-and-needles to come.

Gradually, through the thinning smoke, the real world appeared, and there came the sound of Osa whining with unusual urgency. Nuria looked over her shoulder at Catty but found she'd looked the wrong way. She found herself staring at the edge of the Common, and this made her think that the wish had plucked her up and transported her a few yards for some inexplicable, magical purpose. Where were Catty and the sled? She swept the Common with her gaze, startled to see that the ground was very much closer than it should have been. Osa stood on four tense legs beside the Pillar, which looked rather as if it were sneering.

Then slowly, her heart filled with misgivings she could not name, Nuria looked toward the Well.

A girl leaned against the granite wall. She was rubbing at her temples through a mist of coppery curls. Nuria noted critically that there was a stain on her shabby gray coat. For a moment, just a moment, the girl's name fluttered on Nuria's tongue. She felt as though she'd known the girl all her life, but she couldn't think of her name.

"I have a terrible headache!" said the girl in a clear ringing voice, as though she might sing beautifully. Osa looked at the girl, then slunk away, peering round as though she were searching for somebody.

Then Nuria knew where she'd seen the girl. She'd seen her reflection in the gold-framed mirror over the Winters' mantle, seen her distorted by the copper pot in the Avy's kitchen.

"Nuria!" she said. "Nuria Magdelena."

Nuria looked down and saw what she'd already known she'd see. She examined her body bit by bit, as though she were a patchwork girl, piecing herself together from odd scraps and tatters. She couldn't bear to discover the whole truth at once.

The garnet ring fit loosely on her middle finger; her hands were lying on a bed of white wool. Nuria let her eyes trail down the wool, to its band of ermine, and then still further to the smooth bright button boots, shiny as the day of their purchase. They'd never been used for walking and lay in limp, odd angles on the sled. An expanse of hardened, crusty snow spread out around the sled. Beyond the Common lay the village, the world, the sky.

The Common receded to nothing more than a hard glittering speck, and gravity granted to Nuria a special dispensation from its heavy rule. She drew away from her body to float above the Common, watching the two girls below with nothing more than detached interest. She saw the Pillar's craggy skull, the fringed shawl Agnes wore about her head. She saw Osa creep toward the sled with her tail between her legs, her ears tilted forward into curved question marks. Osa pushed at the dark-haired girl's face with her nose, then heaved her upper body onto the lap on the sled, where she lay with her paws dangling over the other side.

It was Osa's familiar doggy smell, which had always seemed to Nuria like very good fried potatoes, that tugged Nuria gradually toward the ground. She might have been a balloon, her life's air leaking through a small but fatal wound. At the same time, the true horror of her situation rushed over her in a sickening wave, and she grunted as if she'd received a blow to the stomach. She was obliged to sit very still to recover her breath.

"Catty," she said finally. "We have to revoke the wish."

But the copper-haired girl was examining the sole of her shoe. It was imprinted with a pattern of scuffs and scrapes that documented Nuria's particular way of moving through the world, unique as any fingerprint. "I can walk," said Catty slowly, as if she'd just realized that she could now control these shoes, change their pattern and make it her own.

"I take it back!" Nuria tried to cry out, but she'd pitched her new voice too high and had to start again. "Tell me, Agnes! Tell me about taking back the wish!"

"You wouldn't want to do that, would you?" said Agnes. "Not now you've made the Well so happy. It got the wish it was waiting for, you know, and now it can start to melt. Those eggs you talk so much about may even have a chance."

"Tell me!" shouted Nuria.

"One cycle of the moon to repent and call it back."

"Yes, but how? Could I say, *I take back my wish about Catty?*"

"You may use any words that express an intent to take it back," said Agnes, "and you need not actually be at the Well to do so. But Catty must be present with you and, of course, she must revoke it too."

"What about that?" said Nuria. "Do we have to take it back at exactly the same time?"

"If," said Agnes, "within one cycle of the moon—"

"Never mind the moon!" said Nuria sharply. "What if we said it in the same minute?"

Agnes looked at the Well again with the same intent, questioning gaze. "A minute will do fine."

"But I got my wish," said Catty. "Look at me now!"

She dashed around madly, crunching through the crusty snow, breaking Nuria's boots of old habits and training them in new ways. Osa surged forward as though she might leap up and herd Catty into some kind of order. But then she hesitated, and her chest sunk back onto Nuria's lap. Together, they watched Catty run.

But who was really running? It was Catty who decided to plunge across the Common to the embankment, but it was Nuria's muscles that took her there. "Don't leave me!" cried Nuria.

Catty turned around, but she kept dancing in place. "Tell Wilkes to put the sled under the back porch. I'll be along to fetch it."

"It's my sled!" said Nuria. "I just let you ride on it." But if Catty heard, she did not reply; and Nuria's boots took her up the embankment and out of sight.

Long moments passed. "You can't feel anything in a dream," said Nuria, and pinched her calf. There was no pain, just blessed nothingness.

She bit her wrist, then jumped. "Oh," she said slowly, then struck at her leg savagely. She'd never realized Catty had no feeling in her legs.

"Who am I?" she said presently, looking at her hand. It was Catty's hand, but its trembling came from Nuria alone, and the ring, with its flash of garnets, belonged to Nuria too.

"I am Nuria. Nuria Magdelena. I have memories. I live with the Avy. I remember skating. I remember singing."

Catty may have taken her voice, but at least Nuria had the memory of singing. Catty didn't know the hundreds, maybe thousands, of songs Nuria knew. Catty didn't know all twelve verses of "Darling Johnny."

> And it's where have you gone to, my Johnny, my darling?
> Where's your spirit gone roaming, my darling, my ain?
> They say that the maid from the city's bewitched you:
> How I wish you'd return to your own self again!

She wore Catty's skin, but she was not Catty.

"I am Nuria," she said out loud. "The Avy loves me. I love the Avy. He sings. . . ."

Tonight there'd be no singing with the Avy.

She couldn't bear the thought, and she willed her mind to float away from her body again. But it stayed obstinately with the rest of her, which was bound into Catty's muscles, stitched firmly inside her skin.

"I can play the describing game so that the Avy nods and says, 'Yes! Yes!' I can tell him about the sky on the day I made my wish. I can tell him it was a smoky opal lit from inside by sparks of red and green and blue."

She stared into the iridescent sky, and as the afternoon trembled between day and dusk, the sky dimmed and its opal lights went out.

What Child Is This?

Nuria sat very still at supper that night. She felt like a tiger, immensely powerful and hugely furious, but twitching only the tip of her tail. Her cage was strong and carefully locked, so what was the point of doing anything else?

Miss D'Estuffier opened her mouth. Mr. Winter opened his, too. A morsel of chicken disappeared behind Miss D'Estuffier's pretty lips. Her jaw worked up and down. Mr. Winter patted his mouth with a napkin. How strange it was that people shoveled food into their mouths, and poured talk out of their mouths, and none of it meant anything.

"You haven't eaten a bite," said Mr. Winter.

"I did so eat a bite," said Nuria, "but it doesn't taste the same." Catty's tongue was different. It shrank away at the taste of salt, and now she couldn't find that place where sharp cheese explodes with a wonderful *ping!*

"I won't go to Abbyburgh!" she yelled suddenly, surprising herself as much as Bertha, who gasped and dropped a glass.

Mr. Winter's fork clattered to his plate, and both he and Miss D'Estuffier stared at her in astonishment. It seemed that the high ceiling leaned its curved shoulders closer, also astonished at this new sound in its quiet existence.

"She doesn't want to go to Abbyburgh," said Mr. Winter, obediently passing Nuria's message to Miss D'Estuffier.

"So I hear," said Miss D'Estuffier, looking at Nuria with a sudden wariness as though she might have glimpsed the tiger inside. "We do everything for your own good, Catty dear."

"You do?" said Nuria with a sudden equal wariness. That's just what Aunt Hortense had said when she shipped Nuria off to live with her other cousins, who after two months had turned around and shipped her back.

Miss D'Estuffier shook her head. "Now do you see, Mr. Winter, why she needs the civilizing effects of a metropolis like Abbyburgh? She's been running wild too long."

"I'm hardly running," said Nuria. Behind her someone laughed, then turned it into a cough.

"That's quite enough, Bertha."

Nuria slipped her hand into her pocket and felt the comforting circle of her mother's ring, warm from the heat of her body.

"Can't we enjoy Bishop Mayne while we're here?" said Mr. Winter pleadingly, leaning over the table toward Nuria. "You wanted to go to the caroling tonight."

The caroling. Nuria had almost forgotten about the Christmas Eve caroling on the Common. The Avy had spoken of it this morning, but this morning seemed a lifetime ago. Oh Avy, Avy, she thought, pressing at a lump of misery just below her breastbone. She'd never be able to sleep without singing with him, or playing the describing game.

"What do you have there?" said Miss D'Estuffier with her old easy charm.

"Where?"

Miss D'Estuffier leaned forward, bringing into Nuria's field of vision three sharp hairpins that skewered her hair in place. "There, on your finger."

"Nothing!" said Nuria and whipped her hand beneath the table. That was the worst thing she could have done, of course. It made her look so furtive, as though she'd stolen her own garnet ring.

"Come, come," said Miss D'Estuffier, holding out her slender hand. The palm was tinged with yellow.

Nuria looked at Mr. Winter, who was rubbing at his bald spot worriedly. He was so mild and obedient that Nuria despised him.

"That's Nuria's ring, I think," said Miss D'Estuffier.

"She lent it to me," said Nuria. "For our play."

"You'd best give it to me," said Miss D'Estuffier.

Nuria did not move.

"Best give it to her," said Mr. Winter.

Nuria dropped the ring into Miss D'Estuffier's palm. "Don't lose it!" she cried, watching those long, elegant fingers swallow it up.

Miss D'Estuffier slipped the ring into her pocket, and after a little silence, Nuria said, "The Princess has concluded her royal repast and is waiting for her escort to the ball."

Mr. Winter rose and bowed. "The midnight hour is upon us," he said, surprising Nuria that he knew the language of fairyland. "Your carriage awaits."

But the carriage had to wait a long time. Nuria was lashing her tiger-tail by the time they were ready to go. She couldn't stand it; it all took so long, and it was all so fussy. The way she had to wear a sweater beneath her coat. The way Mr. Winter buttoned her boots with slow, careful fingers.

She almost slapped his hands aside when he tried to button her coat. "I can do it myself!"

She couldn't walk herself, however, and Mr. Winter carried her through the front door. But then he suddenly hissed and whirled around, shielding Nuria with his shoulder. Osa stretched her long, black body from the porch.

"My wolf!" cried Nuria. "The royal wolf!"

But Mr. Winter stood as though paralyzed, clutching her so tightly it hurt.

"It's only the Avy's dog," said Nuria, disgusted at his cowardice. She tried to wiggle her shoulders loose of his grip.

"Will the Avy's dog be so good as to step aside?" said Mr. Winter. But it was he who stepped carefully around Osa, then carried Nuria high in his arms as Osa danced beside them to the carriage.

Nuria pressed her forehead to the cold window, enduring the headache it gave her in order to see Osa following them. But the night was dense and black, and she could see only small circles of light from the carriage lanterns, which glazed the snow as they trembled over the road. The world wheeled upside-down when they reached the Common, the ground turning into the sky as scores of Christmas torches dipped and winked in the night.

A crowd was already gathered around Father Michael, who led the caroling. Light snow shimmered in the torchlight like silver glitter eased through the finest of sieves.

One side of this charmed circle curled apart from itself and a dark shape broke off from the night. It shot past the fire and hurled itself onto Nuria's lap.

The impact thrust her against the back of the wheelchair. Mr. Winter shouted out and lunged forward as though to save her.

"Stand back, knave!" cried Nuria, trying to pull Osa onto her lap. A row of cold-flushed faces and fire-lit eyes swung round their way, then turned back again politely, for this was clearly a family argument.

Mr. Winter stopped as though he'd run into a wall. He removed his hat, although the night was cold, and turned it around by the brim.

"Come, Osa!" cried a familiar, gravelly voice, and Nuria's head jerked up to see the Avy coming toward her through the crowd. Catty followed the Avy, but Nuria ignored her, and she barely noticed Osa slipping reluctantly from her lap. Nuria had eyes only for her grandfather, studying him so that at any time she could bring his face into her memory.

He stood straight and walked too briskly for his torch, whose flame flickered in the breeze he made, almost gutting itself in the oil that fed it. His scalp gleamed in the torchlight, his face was satin-hard, like the fragile outer skin of a dried date.

Mr. Winter bowed to the Avy before he put his hat back on. "I've never seen a dog lie in wait all evening for a perfect stranger."

"I may be perfect," said Nuria, "but I'm not a stranger."

"Osa did what?" began the Avy, but he was interrupted by tall Mr. Garvey, the baker, who strode toward them, calling their names in his great booming voice.

"Hey, over there! Father Michael sent me on a mission to find a pretty girl to sing the children's solo. She'd need to be, oh, about eleven years old. Either of you need a job?"

"You sang the children's solo last year," said Nuria to Catty.

"I can't sing it tonight," said Catty.

"You can't?" said the Avy, bringing the torch closer to her face, as though that might illuminate his understanding.

"I can't," repeated Catty, shrugging into the air with her own dancing hands, and Nuria knew with sudden clarity that Catty would sing if she could. She'd never pass up a chance to perform. So it must be that she still couldn't sing. Maybe a voice wasn't something that came along with a body, not like teeth and hair and nails.

"You wouldn't sing with me tonight, either," said the Avy. His torch framed Catty's face with a half-arc of light. "Nuria! You've lost something!"

He stepped closer, and Catty squinted away from the flame. "It's your eyes," he said. "Where are the gold stars in your eyes?"

"Children change so quickly," said Mr. Winter.

"You'll never know how quickly," said Nuria, and then she spoke out before she lost her courage, because what if she was wrong about Catty and her voice?

"I'll sing tonight."

"But Catty," said Mr. Winter, "you're always saying you can't sing."

"But it was Miss D'Estuffier who said it first," said Nuria. "Maybe she's wrong."

"A crown for the singer," said Garvey, producing a black metal circlet with tiny candle holders all around. Nuria felt it sigh onto her head.

"But I want to wear the crown!" Catty pulled off her hat and fluffed her hair as though she'd forgotten that no hat could subdue it for very long. Thousands of individual strands sprang into the air, illuminated by the torchlight like so many copper wires. Catty looked at her fingers as though surprised by a new texture.

"What beautiful titian hair!" said Nuria, intending to be sarcastic but finding she meant it, as though Catty actually owned that hair and might be complimented on it.

It was frightening how easy it was to give her hair away to Catty. She must never forget what was Catty and what was her.

"Nuria!" she whispered, baptizing herself with her own powerful name. "I am Nuria, and Catty will never be me."

There came a whoosh of flame and a sudden brightening as Father Michael threw an armful of pine onto the fire. "O, come all ye faithful," he called, both to catch the crowd's attention and to announce the first song. He blew into his pitch pipe to find the pitch that would most harmoniously serve the crowd's many voices.

> O, come all ye faithful,
> Joyful and triumphant. . . .

Nuria made her mind and body into a dark, still well and sunk deep into herself, searching for her old voice inside this new skin. Her eyes stayed open, but she didn't see Father Michael urging the parishioners on toward Bethlehem. She saw instead a vast, deep darkness for which she had no map, no guide, to help her find her way. She sat patiently in the wheelchair, under her crown, its candles as yet unlit, exploring this uncharted territory. There, in the stillness, she heard a note. Its vibrations shivered down her spine. She echoed it softly and knew she'd found a place where she could start to sing.

The crowd's voice was ragged, staggering through the beginning of the song, but it began to come together as it neared Bethlehem.

> O, come ye,
> O, come ye,
> To Be-eth-le-hem.

But after Bethlehem came the high note, and the crowd hesitated, each person making a different decision on whether to come in on the lower octave, whether to drop out altogether, or whether to sing it boldly and hang the consequences. But Nuria's voice had always liked high places, and this is where she joined in.

> Come and behold him,
> Born the king of angels;
> O, come let us adore him. . . .

Mr. Winter's hand on her shoulder stiffened. "Listen to you!"

"Ssh!" said Nuria. She didn't mean to be rude, but she was concentrating fiercely, casting gossamer spider lines, hoping they'd stick to bits of her true self; and as they sang "Silent Night," then "The First Noel," she began to weave the real Nuria, the old Nuria, into this new body.

Father Michael approached her with a burning taper. "Do you need me to find you a note?" He touched the taper to the candles in her crown.

"I have my own note." Nuria made her skull into a cathedral with high echoing ceilings of clear cut glass, and from that cathedral she sang her song into the night.

> What child is this, who laid to rest,
> On Mary's lap is sleeping?

She sang it through with ease and certainty. She imagined her voice spinning into the sky, an arching crystalline bridge to the stars, and the crowd did not wait for the end to begin applauding.

Later, Nuria sat sideways in the carriage, her feet dangling out the open door, as she waited for Wilkes and Mr. Winter to strap the wheelchair to the top. The Avy and Osa stood on the edge of the light-circle cast by the carriage lamps. Osa's ears were turned like antennae toward the carriage, but the Avy's command of "Stay!" held her like an invisible leash.

"Osa!" called Nuria softly from the highest place in the glass-roofed cathedral of her skull, hoping the sound wouldn't reach the ears of the Avy, or of Mr. Winter or Wilkes, tuned as they were to a world in a lower key.

"Osa!"

A black shape streaked across the snow and hurled itself through the door. Nuria felt a moment of real fear as she fell backward onto the seat. This is what Little Red Riding Hood must have felt, surprised at her grandmother's bedside by great white teeth and slavering jaws. But then a wolfish tongue curled into Nuria's ear and began to lick it into Osa's own idea of cleanliness, and Osa's familiar fried-potato smell overpowered the too-clean leather smell of the carriage. Nuria wrapped her arms around Osa's neck, although her heart was still beating faster than it should.

"Osa!" cried the Avy. "Come! Come away at once!" Osa jumped out of the carriage but looked over her shoulder at Nuria as though there were a band of elastic connecting them, and she might snap back at any moment.

The Avy ordered Osa to stay with a silent palm-out gesture. He ran to the carriage and looked up into Nuria's eyes, past the thick black lashes that had once belonged to Catty. Whatever words of apology had been forming on his lips now followed the downward motion of his jaw, which dropped open, making a black hole in his face.

"What magic is this?" said the Avy. "You have gold stars in your eyes."

Ask me, Avy! thought Nuria desperately, remembering how the Avy had been able to talk to her about his wish because she already knew about it. If he asked her if she was Nuria, he would know about her wish and then the Well would let her speak.

The Avy never once let his gaze flicker from her eyes. "I'm a crazy old man, you know, and that's what you must tell yourself if you don't understand what I'm about to say."

His voice trembled, and he held out his hands. "Nuria?"

Nuria began to answer him with her own hands, but just as she was uncurling her fingers so she could lay her palms on his, a terrible heaviness flowed down her arms. She couldn't move them; they were cold and still, weighted with liquid stone.

The Well would not let her speak. The Avy would have to know already about her wish before they could break the rule of silence.

The Avy's arms fell heavily to his sides. "Forgive me please, Catty. Remember what I said about the crazy old man."

"There was no real sunset today, Avy," said Nuria, pleading with him to know her. "The sky was a cloudy opal with sparks of color glittering through. The sparks flickered one by one, and then they died."

He opened his mouth as though to say something, but Mr. Winter walked round the side of the carriage, announcing cheerfully that they were ready. The Avy did not speak, and Nuria could not, so there was nothing to stop Mr. Winter from tucking the lap robe around Nuria as though she were his little girl. There was nothing to stop him from closing the carriage door between her and the Avy and driving her away.

Christmas

Nuria woke at five minutes to midnight, a victim of her own helpless habit of waiting for the smoke-face. But maybe she hadn't slept at all. How could she, when the Avy hadn't come to check on her? She smelled ironing and starch, and her shoulder sank into unaccustomed softness. The darkness pressed in at her, and she squeezed her eyes shut, preferring the friendly darkness she made herself. It was midnight now; the parlor clock struck the hour. The sound filled her with a kind of despair, and she wrapped the pillow round her ears.

It was either the clock, or her dreaming of the clock, that woke her next. Light leaked in around the curtains, and she slid her cheek to the edge of the pillow. The pillow was wet. If Nuria had been a storybook heroine, she would have tried to jump out of bed on this first confused waking, forgetting where she was and what had happened. But she was no heroine, and she stayed as still as a mummy in a tomb. She knew with dreadful clarity that she was in Catty's house, wrapped in Catty's body. She didn't even try to move her toes. There was no use.

"I want the Avy," she said finally, then bit the inside of her mouth, for she couldn't let another piece of herself slip away in another salty tear.

The door opened a crack and Bertha crept in, carrying two steaming buckets. She knelt and poured a clunkety pile of coal into the grate with a little brass shovel. Bertha tipped the hot water into a washtub, and some new caution kept Nuria quiet until Bertha turned around and met her eyes. A bucket clattered to the hearth.

"Mercy! I thought you'd be asleep, late as you were out last night."

"The clock woke me," said Nuria.

"We'll wait a bit for the water to cool. And then we'll wash your hair, shall we?"

"Wash my hair!" said Nuria, horrified. "I hate washing my hair." She put a hand to her head, thinking of the endless snarls and tangles that had to be combed out at washing time. But her fingers met a sleek waterfall and leapt away like startled birds.

"Why, you never said so before, Miss Catty."

"There are lots of things I haven't ever said," said Nuria restlessly. "What do you do for Christmas, Bertha? Do you leave out food for the Christ Child?"

"Not for Him," said Bertha. "For the Christmas fairies. And we leave the door open a crack so's they can slip in. Don't tell Miss D.," she added hastily. "You know how she doesn't like the doors open and such."

"Oh, I'm the queen of secrets," said Nuria bitterly. "I won't ever tell."

Bertha looked into her bucket as though she'd lost something. "I beg your pardon, Miss, but there's something different about you today."

Nuria leaned out from the shadow of her canopy, hoping Bertha could see the real Nuria peering from beneath Catty's skin. Bertha reached out as though to cup Nuria's chin in the heavy framework of her palm. But the moment passed, and Bertha's hand fell back into the dark folds of her skirt.

"You surely do look different," she said at last. "There's something around the eyes."

That's what the Avy had said last night. That her eyes were different. Windows to the soul, she thought, remembering something she'd once heard. The Well wouldn't let her speak, but maybe her eyes could speak for her.

"What do you leave for the fairies?" she said at last. "Almonds and tangerines?"

"Oh no," said Bertha. "The fairies have a sweet tooth, or so I've been told. We leave sugar cookies and pralines and a dish of watered chocolate."

"Do they eat it?"

"Of course," said Bertha, looking at Nuria cautiously, and Nuria could tell she was trying to decide whether Nuria really believed in St. Nicholas and Christmas fairies, or whether they had reached a silent, friendly agreement to play a game of make-believe.

"You put out food for the fairies, and then what?"

"There's a little rhyme we say."

"Just like we sing the 'Giving Song,'" said Nuria.

"What's that, Miss?"

"I was thinking," said Nuria, "that you'll need the services of the world's expert on fairies." She jabbed her thumb to her chest. "That's me."

"We'd be grateful for your help, Wilkes and I. Only a child's as cunning as those fairies."

"And what's more," said Nuria in her grandest voice, "I relinquish you from your duty of giving me a bath."

This Bertha would not permit altogether, but she did let Nuria go without a hair wash. Then Nuria had to submit to two layers of petticoats, and also to stockings.

"Most young ladies don't get silk stockings," said Bertha when Nuria grumbled, "or silk dresses."

"Most young ladies aren't me!" said Nuria, but despite herself, she reached out to touch the pale blue dress, with its silly, wide sash, that Bertha held in front of her. The dropped waist ended with a crisp bow, and the skirt was a mass of careful little pleats.

"You'll ruin it, Miss!" cried Bertha, as Nuria crunched a handful of the skirt into her fist.

Bertha was red-faced and perspiring by the time

Wilkes came to collect Nuria for breakfast. "Fair exhausted me," she said, wiping her hands on her apron as Wilkes scooped Nuria into his arms. She closed the door behind them with a little bang.

"Where's my wheelchair?" demanded Nuria. It was humiliating to be carried like a baby, humiliating the way her useless feet in their useless blue-strap slippers dangled limply over Wilkes's arm.

"Dining room, Miss," said Wilkes, sounding surprised, and moments later he was settling her into her place at the table.

"Canary for breakfast?" said Nuria, looking at the canary's cage standing before her. It was covered by a cloth, just as the Avy covered bread to keep it hot. "Bound to be delicious."

"The others will be coming soon," said Wilkes, sighing deeply as a hint that he might be tired after carrying her all that way. Then he bowed and left her alone in the room.

Out went Nuria's hand and plucked the cover from the cage. "One must see one's breakfast, after all." The canary blinked as though he were not accustomed to the light, and Nuria noticed a curious yellow glaze covering his eyes, like a second eyelid made of onionskin.

"You don't sing much, do you canary?" said Nuria. She glimpsed herself in the sideboard mirror, her reflection striped by the bars of the cage. Despite what Bertha had said about her looking different, the reflected face was so like Catty's that she stretched open her mouth and eyes to see if she could catch a glimmer of Nuria inside.

"If I were home now, I'd be singing. Did you sing on Christmas day, canary, in your island home?" Nuria imagined the canary waking up on Christmas under a huge fern, the sun sifting through the fronds in little streams. "I suppose it's dangerous out there," she said doubtfully, thinking of snakes. "But wouldn't anything be better than this?"

The canary was silent.

"There are spiders in my cottage," Nuria continued. "But of course they're not dangerous. They make their webs between the beams and the roof of my loft, and I stare at them in the morning. There are patches of cobwebs there too, like little gardens."

Her voice trailed off in mild surprise. She'd not realized so many of these homely details had passed through the window of her eye to sink into memory. She tapped her head a little to shake other buried treasures to the front.

The mirror turned suddenly dark, and Nuria looked out through the bars of the cage. Behind her own striped reflection, she saw the sharp V of Miss D'Estuffier's bodice and the sober tweed of Mr. Winter's sleeve.

Strong fingers gripped Nuria's shoulder. "You must never," said Miss D'Estuffier, with even emphasis, "not ever, take the cover from the canary's cage. That is for me alone to do. The drafts will make him sick, and if he were to die, it would be your fault, and you would be a wicked girl."

"Oh surely, Miss D'Estuffier," began Mr. Winter, but the pointed bodice turned and a pale hand appeared on the dark jacket.

"Her judgment and manners are deteriorating, Mr. Winter. That grubby Nuria is a bad influence."

"She's not grubby," cried Nuria. "Look at her beautiful titian hair!"

"Deceitful, too," said Miss D'Estuffier, just as if Nuria hadn't spoken. "There are a few little items missing from about the house, and I'm inclined to suspect her."

"Not her!" cried Nuria wildly. "If anyone's deceitful, it's . . ." But she bit off her words. What could she possibly say? *If anyone's deceitful, it's Catty.* They all thought she was Catty.

"Exactly so," said Miss D'Estuffier ominously. "Consider, Mr. Winter, that it might rub off."

"When Catty sang last night," said Mr. Winter, "you could have knocked me over with a feather. She says it was Nuria who taught her."

"That does not change the problem," said Miss D'Estuffier crisply. "The sooner we're back in Abbyburgh, where children are brought up to be civilized, the better."

The pointed bodice shifted and came to rest just over Nuria's head. "None of those sullen looks now, Miss. Young ladies should smile." Miss D'Estuffier stooped to demonstrate with a little grimace. "Smile!"

Nuria closed her eyes and stepped back into the heart of memory where she knew she'd find a faithful image of the cottage. She looked up and saw the Avy's skis and two pairs of snowshoes stowed above the sitting-room rafters. She examined the dark knotholes in the kitchen's light satiny wood, marveling at their concentric circles. She saw the dark wood of her loft, so rough it bristled with little hairs like the outside of a coconut.

A light hand touched her shoulder. "Are you ill, Catty?" Mr. Winter had knelt to the level of her ear.

No, Nuria wasn't ill, but as soon as Mr. Winter said his daughter's name, Catty stepped into Nuria's head, straight into Nuria's mind-picture of the cottage. Nuria squeezed her eyes, but that only locked Catty in for good. Maybe Catty was playing Pidalo Pom with the Avy, maybe she'd choose the "Giving Song." Maybe Nuria was wrong that Catty couldn't sing.

"Come Catty, let's open the Christmas gifts." Mr. Winter's voice was pleading. "The morning's hardly begun."

"I don't want any gifts," whispered Nuria. "I just want to go to bed."

Voices came and went, but she noticed mostly the

smells. At first there was Mr. Winter's clean, faintly spicy smell, with occasional whiffs of Miss D'Estuffier's violet scent. But when Mr. Winter called for Bertha, a new smell of starch laced faintly with cinnamon came to tuck her into bed.

"Sleep well," it whispered, stroking her hair from her face.

"Wake me up when you put out food for the fairies," Nuria whispered back. "But I'm not going to sleep."

"Of course not," said Bertha.

Nuria wanted to announce that she meant it, that she might never sleep again because how could the Avy come to check on her? But her words were glued to the roof of her mouth, and despite all her good intentions, she quickly fell into a deep and dreamless place.

It was also Bertha who came in to shake her out of sleep and back into the pale-blue pleated silk. "You slept all the day through," she said. "We'll have to hurry just a bit, for the fairies come at twilight, you know. The praline's set to cool and the sugar cookies are baked. You come try one for me. I never know how the baking will turn out in that newfangled contraption."

The contraption turned out to be a terrifying stove, huge and gleaming black, fueled with gas instead of wood or coal. The pan of cookies sat on top. "The world's expert on fairies declares them a success," said Nuria, the dark taste of cinnamon melting on her tongue. "Fairies don't like them too sweet."

Wilkes opened the back door a crack for the fairies and put a finger to his lips. "Quiet's the word on this, Miss Catty. The Mistress will have our heads if she thinks we let cold air into the house."

Nuria spat on her finger and crossed her heart. "Neither the rack nor the wheel will drag it out of me." The bell above the door jumped, then jangled insistently, and Wilkes and Bertha looked at each other.

"Mr. Winter will be wanting the champagne now," said Bertha.

"Her Royal Highness, truer to say," said Wilkes.

Bertha shushed him. "Will you wait here, Miss Catty? We shan't be long."

"The fairies and I will wait," said Nuria, eyeing the crack in the door, an idea taking shape in her mind. Osa had been waiting for her last night, then followed her to the Common. She was sure to be waiting again tonight, and she was big enough to pull the sled that was also waiting beneath the porch. It was Nuria's sled, the very one Catty had left her stranded on yesterday, after the wish. For the first time, Nuria approved of her wide sash. It would make a fine harness.

Wilkes and Bertha left Nuria leaning her cheek against the door. She heard the wind scratch at the lock, felt it breathe through the crack. Nuria pulled at the doorknob, and the wind gained confidence and pressed on through with a cold and bony shoulder. Nuria smiled to think of it racing through the house, flattening to pass under the parlor door and give Miss D'Estuffier a cold kiss on the neck.

Fairies or no fairies, she was not going to wait. She was going to force her way into the twilight and through the blowing snow. And though gravity had declared war upon her and turned into an enemy, she intended to make a sturdy fight all the way up the mountain to see her Avy. She opened the door.

Oh, it was cold out there, bitter and cold. The wind screamed about her ears and tore inside her dress as though it would flay the flesh from her bones. She tipped herself out of the wheelchair by hanging onto the outside doorknob, which was so cold her warm hand almost stuck to the brass. Her weight made the door swing open, and she rode with the motion for a moment, then fell. She was already out of the wheelchair, almost out the door, and she scrabbled with her arms to drag her legs over the threshold.

The wind raised the hairs along Nuria's arms, but it was mostly fear that raised the hairs at the back of her neck. She was afraid of her journey into the dark, lit only by a new-moon sliver of light. But she was more afraid of what might happen if she didn't reach the cottage before the singing time began.

She was afraid Catty might claim the Avy for her own.

Nuria slid on her backside to the porch steps. The silk slid easily over the snow, and she found herself thinking it was too late to go back. The dress was ruined now. The whipping snow all but blinded her. She squeezed her eyes and saw, in the last light, Osa's shaggy, snowy form at the edge of the pond.

Nuria made her skull into the echoing glass cathedral of last night and called from the highest place she could find. But Osa sat as though rooted to the ground. Nuria kept calling, still calling, her voice as high and piercing as the wind itself, calling only because she liked the feel of Osa's name in her mouth. The wind had carried away her voice, and she'd lost all hope that Osa could hear.

"Osa! Osa!" Calling still, sliding down the steps, rolling off the bottom step and into the snow.

And if she'd thought it cold before . . . if hell were made of ice, she thought, this would be it. The notion warmed her as she rolled, her pale blue dress freezing before it even got wet; and as she rolled down the slope to Osa, she thought of fiery icicles leaping at her, scorching her skin to a frozen white.

She dragged her thoughts from fire and ice by picturing Osa waiting patiently, looking perhaps at the squares of filtered light, wondering which was Nuria's window. Nuria stopped for a moment and pretended she was Osa, wrapped in thick black fur, then rolled onto her back to look up at the house. The first floor blazed with lights, and when she squinted her eyes against the stinging snow, the colors melted into an aurora borealis.

The frantic wind slammed snow from the ground onto tree trunks, exposing battered yellow grass, like sand.

I'm in the desert, thought Nuria. Boiling hot in the desert, in a sandstorm. Look at those ripples and ridges in the sand. That sunken bit's a watering hole for a camel. I'll rest there on my way to the oasis.

Osa became mixed up in her mind with the oasis, and on and on she rolled. She didn't stop at the watering hole but kept on her way, leading a train of camels laden with musty spices and fragrant oils and silks for cloistered maidens, silks so fine you could pull them through a lady's ring.

The sandstorm grew fiercer. We'll take shelter at the oasis, thought Nuria. The camels are weary. She rolled through the gritty sand, and when she finally reached the oasis she could not, for a long, shuddering moment, make out how Osa had turned into a statue covered with snow.

There was no Osa after all. How could she have thought the angel statue was Osa?

Where was Osa?

"The camels are weary," said Nuria aloud. That was all she could think of to say at this final betrayal.

She liked the phrase and repeated it, and the last thing she saw was the moon as it slipped across the sky.

The Awakening

Mostly it was all darkness. And mostly all silence, too. But sometimes this eternal night was fractured by wheeling points of light; and sometimes, too, words shattered the darkness, swirling about Nuria's ears and floating on her mind.

"Catty! Can you hear us, Catty?"

Yes, she could hear but she did not understand, did not even try, except once when she heard, "The Avy sent a lovely gift, almonds and apricots and tangerines. Very expensive they must have been."

Those were the gifts for the Christ Child! Nuria tried to move her head, tried to open her begging, wanting fingers. Almonds! Apricots! Tangerines!

"Shh! Shh! my honey," said another voice. "Be still."

Be still. Nuria would be still. She could only be still, wrapped in centuries of sleep.

There came the voices again, calling her back. But she was drifting on the current of a warm dark stream, further and further from the world.

"Catty! Catty!" But this was the Avy's voice, crusty and worn with many years of use. Nuria fought against the warm insistence of the stream, against the pinpoint of light that beckoned from the end of her journey. Sing! she wished desperately. Sing! And the Avy, as he often did, must have read her mind.

> And it's where have you gone to, my child, my darling?
> Where's your spirit gone roaming, my darling, my ain?
> They say that the maid from the city's bewitched you:
> How I wish you'd return to your own self again!

She was trapped in layers of night, but she swam toward the song, sinking finally into a sleep that pressed her eyes shut and held her limbs prisoner in heavy warmth.

Nuria opened her eyes. The chandelier spun round and round, not unlike her own brain, suspended in the domed chamber of her skull. A faraway clock struck five strokes. It could be morning or evening. Each was just as dark as the other. She wondered in a dull way how much time had passed.

"Look!" said a voice. "She's awake!" But Nuria had already closed her eyes, spinning into a waking dream of mechanical notes floating down the long tunnel of her ear. How did my music box get here? she thought in a muzzy way.

As she fumbled through the dark labyrinth of sleep, she heard not only the music but also a whoosh and roar, like the sea. Nuria opened one eye, which was squeezed between the mattress and the aching heaviness of her head. She saw a tiny wooden doll and beyond that, the edge of her sheet, heavy with eyelet embroidery.

She opened her other eye. The chandelier was quiet and resigned now, its crystal pendants perfectly still. A shallow, rhythmic breathing floated on the silence. She turned her head, and the rubbing of cheek against pillow released the sweetish smell of the Winters' laundry soap.

"You're awake!" cried Mr. Winter, springing toward the bed, his arms stretched wide to embrace her. But he stopped suddenly and let his hands fall limply to his sides, as though she might disintegrate with a single touch.

"Open the curtains!" said Nuria. She had to see the moon. How much time before her month to revoke the wish had run out?

"Yes, of course, the curtains," said Mr. Winter, looking at her as though he might cry.

"Don't worry. I haven't gone mad, I promise. But I need to look outside."

"This isn't quite how I'd envisioned your awakening," said Mr. Winter, but he was smiling a little, and leaned over to tug at the curtain pull.

Bluish winter light bounced off the icy tree branches, startling the chandelier so that its shadow on the ceiling jumped. There was no moon, nothing but glinting branches against a dull, powdery sky.

"What day is today?" said Nuria.

"New Year's Eve."

"Not New Year's Eve!" And although Nuria hated arithmetic, her brain effortlessly added up the days that had passed. Her journey into the night had cost her a week, seven whole days of the moon's twenty-eight-day cycle. Only three weeks left to revoke the wish. Nuria picked up the little doll and pressed it to her chest. "Sarah," she said. "How did she get here?"

"Nuria told the Avy to give it to you. He says that she's quite altered and no longer cares for her old playthings." Mr. Winter wrapped Nuria's fingers around the music box. "He brought this, too."

She looked at it doubtfully. It looked suddenly humble and homespun, and the sight of it this way made a little hole inside her. She felt a sudden flare of hatred for the library's rich wood paneling, and her fingers faltered on the winding key. Maybe, in this room, the bitter-sweet beauty of "Darling Johnny" would become a limping, shabby thing.

Nuria pushed herself up against the pillows with the heels of her hands and looked over, exhausted from the effort, to see that Mr. Winter was giving her something else.

"Your Christmas presents," he said almost shyly,

placing two boxes on the bed beside her. "You'd never opened your gifts. Somehow that was all I could think about when you were ill."

Nuria watched Catty's fingers pull at the satin bows and peel off layers of filmy tissue. The first box held a porcelain doll, large and rather heavy, with golden candy-floss hair and staring blue eyes that clicked in her head when you laid her back.

"She's very beautiful," said Nuria, which was true, but then she was uncertain where to put her. This doll couldn't take Sarah's place beside her in bed; and Nuria finally laid her carefully on the counterpane, then let Catty's hands reach for the second box.

It was a beautiful big book of *The Snow Queen*. The pictures were on shiny paper, and there was an exciting smell of glue and newness about it.

"I love this!" said Nuria, stroking the shiny paper.

"I thought you might," said Mr. Winter, and there was something about his eager shyness that brought a lump to Nuria's throat. She turned away, looking out again through the window, so he wouldn't see if she cried.

It was the kind of dismal, freezing weather that followed a thaw, with no new snow to hide the raw and dirty ground. When the wind blew, the icy branches rubbed their hands together, making the whoosh and roar she'd thought was the sea.

"Why did you do it?" said Mr. Winter. "Why did you run away, into the snow?"

"Oh, that!" said Nuria, and suddenly everything seemed easy. She'd tell him the whole story, beginning with the Well, and then he'd take her back to the Avy. Her mind formed serious, powerful words, and she began to push them into her mouth so her tongue and lips could give them shape. But suddenly her lungs collapsed and she found herself gasping for air.

"I want to go to the Common," she said at last, silently cursing the Well and its rules. "On Twelfth Night, to put branches in the fire. I want to be like Nuria and do things that regular children do." Let Mr. Winter think she'd rushed into the night to try to be like Nuria, to skate and sled and make angels in the snow.

"But you've been so ill," said Mr. Winter.

"And another thing. I want to be here, in Bishop Mayne, for the Revels."

"Miss D'Estuffier thinks we should return to Abbyburgh as soon as possible," said Mr. Winter uncertainly.

Nuria spoke to him slowly and clearly as though he were either very old or very young. "If we go back before the Revels, I'll lie in bed and never eat and never open my eyes again." She slid down the pillow and closed her eyes and plugged her ears with her fingers.

The next few days seemed like many days, with many muddled awakenings followed by sudden plunges into sleep. Each time she woke up, she worried about where the moon was in its cycle. Once she started to ask what day it was and ended up asking for olives. At first she tried to keep count of her odd fits of sleep, but the numbers slipped through her memory like shadows; and some alert part of her knew that she, in her illness, no longer slept to the rhythm of the spinning earth.

When Nuria really awoke at last, it was daytime. The curtains were drawn open, framing a thick, grayish day with swirling snow. She lay still for a moment, investigating the new clearness in her head. Something dug into her shoulder, and she fished into the bed-clothes, then rolled over, holding Sarah above her face. There was a heaviness beside her, and she poked at it with her elbow. It was the porcelain doll. Bertha knelt at the hearth, raking out the cinders.

"It's Sleeping Beauty!" Nuria cried out suddenly, and smiled when poor, startled Bertha whipped her head around. "Awake at last!"

"You seem a deal better, Miss," said Bertha, straightening her cap.

"Where's the prince with my olives?" Nuria pushed herself to a sitting position and bounced up and down. "What's today?"

"Mr. Winter said you were to be kept quiet."

Nuria made sure her smile showed all of her teeth. "Tell me the date or I'll thrash about in my illness and fall off the bed."

"Illness, my foot!" said Bertha. "It's January second."

"Four days until Twelfth Night," said Nuria, and her new clear brain told her why she had to go to the Twelfth Night celebration. Catty would be there, and Nuria had to talk to Catty, try to convince her. . . .

"Bertha, how would you get someone to say something they didn't want to say?"

"Beg pardon, Miss?"

It was impossible, of course. Catty would never say anything to revoke the wish. Nuria snatched up Sarah and to her own surprise, hurled her at the chandelier. The crystal pendants tinkled weakly. Nuria's nose prickled, but she was in no danger of crying. Her eyes were dry and very hot.

"The throne room's closed for the day," she said in the acid voice Aunt Hortense had most hated. "The Princess desires to be left in peace."

But Bertha was not Aunt Hortense. There was a rather long silence while Nuria stared at the chandelier, which still trembled. "What you want is a change," said Bertha. "It's not natural for a child to lie in bed all day. I know of a little place you might want to visit. The broom closet, up front. Seems two elves have made a home there."

Nuria did look at her then, but Bertha held up a finger. "Your secret's safe with me, as I'm the only one who uses the closet. Your father and Her Highness are talking so hard they'll never know you've come and gone."

"The Princess graciously accepts the assistance offered," said Nuria. "And she is most pleased."

She hadn't thought of Lace Dappled Grove for what seemed a very long time. But now that Bertha had reminded her, Nuria remembered all the fun she'd had with Catty, hiding in their secret place, writing the play of *The Snow Queen*. Maybe she'd finish the play herself. That would show Catty. She'd write Catty an absolutely terrible part.

"What was that you said earlier, Miss?" said Bertha. "Get someone to say something they don't want to say?"

These were the words Nuria had said just minutes ago, but she heard them now in Bertha's mouth as if for the first time. "Bertha, I hereby elevate you to Royal Philosopher!" she said, startled into an astonishing idea. She wouldn't write Catty a terrible part. She'd write her a wonderful part. A terribly wonderful part. If Nuria were clever enough, Catty would say something while she was acting in the play to revoke the wish, and she'd never even know what she was doing.

"The Princess requests further assistance. She'll need help sewing a costume for a Snow Queen."

As if in answer, Bertha scooped Sarah from the floor and tossed her into the air. Nuria's hand snapped out, and there was Sarah, wrapped in her fingers.

"You're fast," said Bertha. "I'll be back with the wheelchair."

Lace Dappled Grove was just as they'd left it. The

lace shawl cast the same magnified shadow against the wall, and the jewels shimmered when the candle was lit. The sugar-water tea had left a sugar coating in the teacups, rough as a dog's tongue. Nuria sniffed at one of the cookies in the cookie tin. It was stale. Despite the hum of voices from the parlor next door, she felt very safe and private in her own secret hideaway, until from out of the hum came a single word.

"Nuria," she heard, and then again: "Nuria."

Nuria put her ear against the wall to hear better.

"Dreadful influence," Miss D'Estuffier was saying. "Before she met Nuria, would Catty ever have run into the snow like that? And the canary!"

Then came Mr. Winter's voice. "She's only a child. She couldn't know the drafts would kill the creature."

"That's Nuria's fault, too," said Miss D'Estuffier. "Catty knows better than to leave the door open."

I knew the canary was going to die, thought Nuria. It came from being covered up all the time. She felt very remote from herself, remembering how on Christmas day the canary was already closing himself off behind opaque yellow lids.

"But Catty wants to be in the Revels so much," said Mr. Winter.

"In my opinion," said Miss D'Estuffier, "we shouldn't even consider exposing her to Nuria."

Exposing her to Nuria. Just as if she were some kind of disease.

"She taught Catty to sing," said Mr. Winter. "You should have heard Catty on Christmas Eve." Then he added, his voice polite as ever, but with a kind of pointed emphasis, "And you were the one who told her she couldn't carry a tune."

There was a silence, and Mr. Winter spoke again. "And what's the harm in staying in Bishop Mayne for the Revels?"

"What harm!" said Miss D'Estuffier. "Postpone our departure to Abbyburgh so she can associate with that light-fingered girl? Mr. Winter, I hadn't wanted to tell you this, but I feel I must divulge my worst suspicions. When I returned that little ring to the Avy, neither he nor his granddaughter could explain how Catty came to have it in her possession. I'm afraid some of Nuria's habits have rubbed off."

"You think she stole the ring?" said Mr. Winter.

"I think she stole the ring."

"That would be serious indeed," said Mr. Winter. "But let's not judge her too hastily. We'll keep an eye on her, now that her health's improving, and give ourselves a little space to decide."

"I bow to your judgment as her father," said Miss D'Estuffier.

Nuria squeezed her eyes shut and waited for Bertha to come fetch her. Lace Dappled Grove would never feel the same again, snug and warm, tucked safely away from the world. The conversation she'd just heard echoed through her memory. *Exposing her to Nuria. Light-fingered girl. Drafts would kill the creature.* And then a picture of the canary came into Nuria's mind. He was lying on his back, his legs stuck stiffly into the air, and this picture led to another picture, so terrifying that Nuria opened her eyes to blot it out.

"The Avy isn't dead, is he?" she whispered. "He can't die before I go home."

And there she sat, her eyes open wide, waiting beside the sugar-coated teacups and stale cookies, for Bertha to take her back to her room.

Twelfth Night

Nuria woke up the next day hating everything. She hated the high starched collar of her nightgown because it scratched her neck. The rest of her skin itched too, as though it were stretching here, shrinking there, trying to accommodate something new inside. She hated the hot chocolate that came on her breakfast tray. The smell made her gag, and she pushed the cup away. "Eggs in chocolate!" she said, watching it tumble and spill. "A delicious new dish."

But then she picked up the cup and placed it carefully on the saucer. "Sorry! Sorry!" she told Bertha, because if she didn't act like Catty, all prissy clean and goody-goody, Mr. Winter might agree to return to Abbyburgh, and then she'd never revoke the wish.

But she could keep on hating quietly, and so she hated the tablecloth on the parlor table where she sat now. It was white and silky-smooth, except for a circular mark left by the canary's cage. She wrote "Kai" on the blank page that yawned in front of her, then drew two parallel curly lines beneath. She hated her idea for making Catty say something in the play to revoke the wish. It meant Catty got to play Gerda, and Nuria had to play Kai. But it was the only thing that might work. When Gerda found Kai at the end of the play and saw how cold and heartless he'd become, she could wish he was the way he'd been before. And if Nuria was Kai in the play, and the Well changed her back to the way she was before . . .

She had to find the right words for Gerda to say.

"Be who you were before!" Nuria scribbled it out. Too obvious.

"I wish you hadn't changed."

She scribbled over that too, then poked the nib of the pen into her index finger. A bead of ink trembled on her fingertip, which she smeared into her skin, then rubbed the rest on the tablecloth.

"Such a mess, Catty darling!"

Nuria jumped at Miss D'Estuffier's voice. Her elbow hit the ink, and although the next moment stretched into an eternity, Nuria wasn't quick enough to catch the bottle before it toppled. She watched a great black stain eat its way over the tablecloth and bite into the white circle where the canary had spent his last silent days. Nuria whisked her paper out of the path of the ink, then swiveled round to look up at Miss D'Estuffier.

"Sorry! Sorry!" said Nuria for the second time that day. She'd never apologized so much in her whole life.

"Accidents will happen," said Miss D'Estuffier with her playful, enchanting smile.

"I didn't steal that garnet ring!" said Nuria suddenly, desperately. "Really I didn't."

Miss D'Estuffier tapped at her teeth with a fingernail, smiling all the while she stared at Nuria with round blue eyes. "Oh, I know that," she said at last. Ink dripped off the tablecloth and splashed onto the carpet. "But someone's been listening at doors. Naughty girl."

"You're lying to my papa about me!" said Nuria, shocked. "Why do you want him to believe I'd steal?"

"To go back to Abbyburgh, of course," said Miss D'Estuffier.

Nuria stared at her without understanding.

"You may as well know, you tiresome girl," said Miss D'Estuffier, expansive now, flinging out her fingers as though throwing caution to the winds. "You see, the longer we stay, the more difficult it is to wean Mr. Winter from the memory of his poor invalid wife. The more difficult it is for him to turn his thoughts to me."

They both looked at the portrait of Catty's mother. "To marry you, do you mean?" said Nuria incredulously.

"Tiresome, but bright enough," said Miss D'Estuffier. "That's it, in a nutshell. Don't look so astonished. Don't you think I can get a proposal out of your father?"

"Why are you telling me this?" said Nuria. "I'm just going to tell him right away."

"I don't think so," said Miss D'Estuffier. "The seed of doubt has been planted. Now that your father thinks you a thief and a liar, he'll never believe your story. Do you think?"

Nuria was forced to shake her head.

"I'm glad we had this little conversation," said Miss D'Estuffier, and she actually reached out and brushed her finger against Nuria's cheek. "At last to speak of it— you have no idea what a burden it is to keep such a thing inside."

"Oh, don't I?" said Nuria sourly. "I know lots of things, things you can't even dream of. I know that my papa loved my mother so much it didn't matter to him she couldn't walk." Nuria said this with complete conviction, although it was only a guess. "He'll never think of you after her. It would take a wish on the Well to make him even look at you!"

Miss D'Estuffier fixed her blue eyes on Nuria's face and stared quietly.

"It's just a joke!" said Nuria, remembering suddenly that outsiders weren't to know about the magic of the Well. "Just a silly children's story. You can't make wishes there, not ones that really come true."

But Miss D'Estuffier was still staring, her very hairpins quivering with interest.

"Attila the Hun for a stepmother," said Nuria, smiling savagely. "What fun! Now leave me alone, I have work to do."

She did not have to pretend to be absorbed in her paper when she looked back down. While her mind had been busy with one problem, the answer to another had sidled up and tapped her on the shoulder. "Darling Johnny," it whispered. Gerda should sing "Darling Johnny."

"Thank you, Avy," whispered Nuria, for the tune of "Darling Johnny" had been running through her mind ever since he'd sung to her when she was ill. Maybe she'd tell him some day. Nuria hummed the song, playing the words through her memory.

> And it's where have you gone to, my Johnny, my darling?
> Where's your spirit gone roaming, my darling, my ain?
> They say that the maid from the city's bewitched you:
> How I wish you'd return to your own self again!

It said what she wanted it to say. How would it sound if she substituted the word "Kai" for "Johnny"? No, no—not "Kai," but "friend."

> And it's where have you gone to, my friend, my darling?
> Where's your spirit gone roaming, my darling, my ain?

Nuria leaned sideways, to the paper she'd saved from the inky mess in front of her, writing as fast as she could to catch the idea before it evaporated.

"My, what's happened to your handwriting?" said Miss D'Estuffier, peering over Nuria's arm.

"Are you still here?" said Nuria, and splayed her fingers over the paper. "Run along now, that's a good little wicked stepmother."

"For the Revels, is it?" said Miss D'Estuffier. Nuria did not have to look up to know she'd be smiling her most enchanting smile. "My poor, dear girl, I very much doubt you'll be here for the Revels."

Mr. Winter did let Nuria go to the Twelfth Night celebration after all. "It's self defense," he said when she thanked him. "You were badgering me to death!"

"Badgering?" she said, surprised, because she thought she'd been so good, so circumspect and honey-tongued, so like prissy-missy Catty Winter.

"Badgering," said Mr. Winter firmly.

She hadn't been outside since Christmas, and the moment they stepped through the door she breathed in deeply. She'd forgotten air could be like this, so fresh and quick and alive in her lungs. Out here her eyes could look anywhere, and they darted from the white plaster sky to the rumpled snow, untidy as if from the tossings and turnings of a troubled night.

"I'll never sleep again!" she cried.

"Never is a long time," said Mr. Winter, but he was smiling as he tucked the lap robes securely around her, for they were going in the sleigh. Wilkes clicked to the horses. There was a bright splash of bells, and off they went.

The Twelfth Night bonfires glowed on the horizon

long before they reached the Common. The sky above the glow was soft and black, although behind her Nuria saw the remains of a lilac-tinted dusk. Soon there came to her the pungent smell of burning pine, and she heard the crackle of fire. But Nuria was really looking for Catty, and some instinct told her to look away from the festivities. She cupped her palms beside her eyes to screen out the distracting light behind, and there, as she'd somehow suspected, was Catty, leaning into the Well, her dangling legs kicking the outside wall.

A wild pulse leapt in Nuria's throat at the sight of her old body. She tugged at Mr. Winter's sleeve. "Take me over there." She pointed because she didn't want to give her name away to Catty. "But then we have to be alone because we have secrets."

"Yes, ma'am!" said Mr. Winter, saluting.

"Please, I mean," said Nuria. "And thank you," she added, as he transferred her in her cocoon of wool to the sled. She kept her eyes fixed on her old body as the sled bumped along to the Well. I must harden my heart, she thought, narrowing her eyes, which gave her a strong, mean feeling. I will not be nice to it! I won't!

"A coin for passage to your heart's desire. That is the first rule."

Catty looked over her shoulder, then slid to the ground. Nuria tugged at Mr. Winter's trouser leg. "My turn to look inside."

"My Lord, Catty!" said Mr. Winter, with just a trace of irritation. "You do pull at me these days."

"A thousand pardons, Master," said Nuria, apologizing for what must be the hundredth time that week. She pressed the palms of her hands together in a little mock bow. Mr. Winter laughed and lifted her up.

Nuria couldn't see anything at first, but then the moon shone out and glimmered off the roses. "Ah!" she said, her voice sighing round the Well in fainter and fainter reflections of itself, echoing finally into extinction.

The Well had started to melt. It had gotten its wish, as Agnes had said, and was done with its little tantrum. The sprays of ice were gone, and the nightingale had emerged from the warm protection of her wing. One of the hummingbirds was sitting on its eggs, although the nest was still white-brown with frost. Drizzles of ice ran down the Well's granite sides, and the water below reflected a bright, full moon. Its eyes were shadowy pockets, staring up at Nuria.

She tapped at Mr. Winter's hand to get down. Two weeks had passed since she'd wished on the Well. The next two weeks would whittle away at the moon, and when the last sliver was gone, she'd have lost her chance to revoke the wish.

Mr. Winter had already stepped away. Catty would not look at Nuria. Possibly she felt as uncomfortable with Nuria as Nuria did with her. "I come with an offering of peace," said Nuria, producing from under her blanket the script of *The Snow Queen*, rolled into a tube and secured with an elastic.

But Catty kept her hands behind her back. "What do you want with me?" she said suspiciously.

"I'm lonely," said Nuria, which felt at that moment like the truest thing she'd ever said.

"I'm lonely too," said Catty. "Nothing is the way I thought it would be."

"At least you have the Avy!" said Nuria.

"But he doesn't love me the way he loves you," said Catty.

Nuria tried not to show how happy this made her. "So let's play together if you're lonely. You can be the princess, O heir to your mother's beauty, most beautiful child in the village."

"But I'm not the most beautiful child in the village," said Catty bitterly.

"You were until we switched bodies," said Nuria.

"I was?"

"Of course you were, but you lost your chance. Now I'm the most beautiful because I'm the only child in the village. You don't count because you live up the mountain."

Nuria did not understand why Catty suddenly turned white and her hands flew to her cheeks. She looked silly, Nuria thought, like a clownish, picture-book picture of horror.

"Is your life passing before your eyes?" she inquired. "It's a good thing you're only eleven, or we'd be here all night."

"Oh, Nuria," said Catty. "I did such a wicked thing."

A kind of liquid relief filled Nuria. Catty realized what a terrible thing she'd done, and now she was going to take back the wish.

"Just tell me when you're ready," said Nuria.

But Catty was not listening. "I never realized it before. It was my wish that made all the children disappear."

"Oh, you're not as wicked as all that," said Nuria. "How could your wish for a stepmother make that happen?"

Now Catty's hands jumped off her face and gripped each other. There were white fingerprints on her cheeks. "I didn't wish for a stepmother," she said crossly. "I wished to be just like my mother, who was the most beautiful child in the village."

"The truth will out," said Agnes, and laughed in a rusty old voice.

Nuria blinked as though she'd stepped into a sudden bright light. It took her a moment to completely understand this startling new idea. The Well had granted Catty's wish to be the most beautiful child in the village by getting rid of all the other children. "That is the stupidest thing I ever heard of!" she said with contempt. "You wasted the one wish in your whole life to be beautiful."

Catty backed away under Nuria's grim gaze. Fat snowflakes caught in her coppery hair, and she looked the very image of a skating girl, lightly frosted and ready for flight. "How would you understand!" she cried. "You've never been compared to your mother. You've never heard the grown-ups whisper. *Beautiful mother. Pity the daughter didn't get her looks.*" Color trembled into Catty's cheeks—Nuria's cheeks, really, but the passion behind it was all Catty's own. "You don't want to be an actress. Actresses have to be beautiful."

"Why didn't you revoke the wish?" asked Nuria.

"I didn't realize what happened until just now," said Catty. "But I couldn't have revoked it anyway. That's when I got so sick. They thought I was going to die, just like my mother."

And it was then, at this mention of Catty's mother, that a white-hot flash of a thought came to Nuria. "You did something even stupider!" she cried, shaking her fist at Catty. "You also wished yourself into that wheelchair."

"What do you mean?" said Catty coldly.

"You wished to be like your mother, your mother couldn't walk, and now you can't either. The Well's probably laughing itself to death right now."

It was a moment Nuria would always remember, shaking her fist at Catty in the moonlight, Catty nodding, and Nuria realizing that Catty had known this all along, while from what seemed a great distance, came the sounds of laughter and the sudden *whoosh!* of burning pine.

"Now you know," said Catty calmly. "They're right when they say the Well makes it hard for you to revoke a wish."

"Because you were so sick," said Nuria, explaining it to herself. "I'm sick too. I'm sick to death of all this. You can go home and have some nice nightmares about it later. But right now let's think about our play for the Revels. If you are a very good girl, I'll tell you how to decide who gets to play Gerda. Do you remember Pidalo Pom?"

"I won the cake last time," said Catty, narrowing her eyes at this recollection.

"And the lucky girl who wins the part of Gerda gets to sing the most be-au-ti-ful song."

> And it's where have you gone to, my friend, my darling?
> Where's your spirit gone roaming, my darling, my ain?

"Not fair," Catty interrupted. "You know I can't sing."

"Miss D'Estuffier says you can't sing," said Nuria. "But she's a liar. She's trying to make your papa believe I stole that garnet ring. She wants to marry him."

Nuria was pleased with the effect of this announcement. "Marry him!" cried Catty with horror.

"And it'll be your fault if she does. Why didn't you just tell them you let me borrow the ring? Now it looks so suspicious."

"I didn't think of that," said Catty. "And I was nervous because your Avy was looking at me in the strangest way."

"We'll show your papa I'm not a bad influence," said Nuria. "I'll be just as good as gold, and you can stand up and sing in front of everyone, just like an actress. You could wear a crown of roses, too."

Nuria invented that last detail on the spot, remembering how Catty had wanted to wear the crown of candles on Christmas Eve. She bowed from her seat, offering the rolled-up script to Catty. "Your scepter, my liege."

But Catty still wasn't convinced. "People will laugh at me."

"Laugh?" said Nuria. "Did anyone laugh when I sang? Of course not! They stamped and shouted wild Huzzahs! and threw gold doubloons at my feet. But maybe I can help you begin."

Nuria turned her memory back to Christmas Eve, retracing the search for her voice in the black night of her inside self. "Close your eyes. There, that's good. Sink down inside yourself. You are dark and deep, and in your heart you hold a trove of precious treasure."

Nuria's voice grew soft and rhythmic as the swing of a hypnotist's watch.

"Now look at your treasure. You have copper coins and gold coins, you have rings set with precious stones. But there's more than that. Look through the piles. What do you see? Look carefully and find your own special treasure. This treasure will become your note."

Nuria hardly dared look at Catty, as though the unseen pressure of her gaze might frighten away Catty's note. She wished the shadows flitting about the fire would be quiet. They looked incapable of so much noise, flat and insubstantial in front of the flames, like dolls cut from black paper.

"Have you found it?" Nuria asked at last.

Catty nodded.

"Your head is an echoing cathedral, all made of glass. Put your treasure in there and let your note stretch out of it, as if you were pouring gold into the night."

Catty moistened her lips, and every bit of Nuria grew watchful and alert. Her fingertips were so tender and receptive that when she stroked the silken lining of her muff, she felt as though there were an eye at the end of each finger. Finally, there came a whispering reed of a voice. "And it's where . . ."

"The gold is streaming out. Let it echo in the cathedral."

"And it's where have you gone to, my friend, my darling?"

Nuria let her jaw drop open. There was nothing wrong with Catty's voice. It sounded just the way she spoke, vigorous and merry. Miss D'Estuffier was lying about everything.

"Where's your spirit gone roaming, my darling, my ain?" Catty opened her eyes.

"The rest of the words are in the script," said Nuria.

"I'm going to be too shy to sing," said Catty.

"Don't let Miss D'Estuffier be right about your singing!" said Nuria. "Just let the gold stream out. We'll practice every day until you can do it perfectly. And by the way, wild Huzzahs! and gold doubloons and all that."

She hoped she didn't sound as grudging as she felt. What had happened here tonight opened the door to a dangerous possibility. "May her blood curdle and her bones pop," said Nuria to herself. "I won't have her singing with the Avy. I won't!"

Pidalo Pom

All the next morning, Nuria sat at the parlor window, puffing great sighs onto the window pane. How was she going to talk to the Avy alone? When could she tell him to let Catty win the part of Gerda? The weather was just as perplexed, unable to make up its mind between snow and rain. Nuria drew a picture of the Avy in the mist she'd made, then leaned into the window, watching the advance and retreat of her breath on the glass.

The real Avy came with Catty toward the house, walking in the slush beside the path to avoid invisible icy patches on the bricks. Osa pranced beside them.

I don't look like that, do I? thought Nuria, seeing Catty's old gray coat, which did not quite cover the plaid skirt, which in turn, did not quite cover the red-flannel knees. The Avy had let down the skirt again—this time as far as it would go—adding yet another horizontal line at the hem where it had been turned up before.

But as it happened, Nuria didn't have to do anything to see the Avy alone. He did it all himself. He turned to Catty when he entered the parlor and said brightly,

"Why don't you run along for a moment. Go play with some of those outfits in that trunk you're always talking about." He looked at Nuria. "You don't mind, do you?"

Nuria shook her head.

"They're dress-ups, not outfits," said Catty, but she was already starting for the door. "I know just what I'll choose."

"Vanity!" said Nuria, watching Catty disappear from the parlor.

"Precisely!" said the Avy. "My Nuria was never vain." And he looked at Nuria with very bright eyes.

He knows! thought Nuria. He knows.

"I knew for certain when she . . ." The Avy pointed in the direction Catty had gone. "Well, it was her idea to let down the skirt; she stitched it all herself. And then, last night, when she said she was tired of the singing game!" The Avy shrugged expressively.

Nuria's heart had turned into a bird, beating madly against the bony cage of her chest.

"I know you're Nuria," said the Avy. "I'll still know— I'll know forever—even if you can't tell me."

Nuria did not realize she was going to speak, but suddenly her words were hanging in the air, destroying her own brief happiness, making the Avy step away from her. "Is this Nuria's idea of a joke? It's not even April Fool's day yet."

Her voice was perfectly shaded to convince the Avy

she was Catty, not Nuria. It was a little distant, a little confused, a little resentful. Even Catty, the actress, couldn't have improved on it.

But it was not Catty's doing, or Nuria's doing, or the doing of any person. It was the Well that had made Nuria speak. It would do everything it could to make sure the wish stayed secret for a month. And the Avy believed her, she could see he did.

"I don't feel old," he said. His hands hung heavily at his sides. Nuria had never seen them still before. "But maybe you never know when you're getting addled. Please accept my apologies. And I've been arrogant, too. I can see I don't know as much about the Well as I think."

"You do so know about the Well," said Nuria, trying to say something to wipe that stricken look from the Avy's face. He looked just the way she felt inside. "You have to know about the Well to make a wish that comes true."

"If my wish came true," said the Avi, "where are all the families?"

"But we came back," said Nuria, meaning Catty and Mr. Winter. "What about that?"

"I have an idea of where my wish went wrong," said the Avy. "I wished to reverse the effect of the wish that took away our children. But there was probably more than one effect of that wish. It made the children disappear, that is true, but I'm willing to bet it also made you leave Bishop Mayne."

"More than one effect," interrupted Nuria, her mind already shaking this idea together with what she already knew. Catty's wish had made Catty into an invalid, which had made Mr. Winter take her to Abbyburgh. That's the effect the Well had reversed, sending Catty back to Bishop Mayne, knowing she might persuade Nuria to make a wish.

The row of bad wishes! thought Nuria, remembering what the Avy had said. Catty's wish-gone-wrong had led to the Avy's wish-gone-wrong, which had led to Nuria's wish-gone-wrong. The Well was fiendishly clever, but Nuria understood it all now. It had even tricked her into thinking the Avy's wish went right. She remembered what Agnes had said about the smoke-face. *Meet the first child to return.* Yes, Catty had been the first child to return, but she had also been the only child.

The Well would be sorry it started this game.

"I want to tell you something secret," she said to the Avy. "We're going to play Pidalo Pom to decide who gets to play Gerda?" She made a question of her statement, and the Avy nodded.

"I want you to let . . ." She swallowed hard before she could say her own name in front of the Avy. "I want Nuria to win the Gerda part. She really wants to be

Gerda, and I . . ." It was fury rather than tears that made her voice tremble so much she could not finish.

"Say!" said the Avy sharply. "What makes you think I can decide who wins at Pidalo Pom?"

"O-ho," said Nuria. "I'm a mind reader. And for you and you alone I'll demonstrate my powers. Do you hear the fairy footsteps of your granddaughter coming down the hall? I predict . . ." Nuria pressed an index finger to each temple. "I predict she'll be wearing pink!"

She had guessed correctly. Catty came in with her most irritating cat-with-cream look, and pulled a footstool to the fireplace so she could see her dress in the mirror above the mantle. Mr. Winter followed, knocking at the molding to announce his presence. Polite as always, Nuria thought, grinding her teeth.

But it was an exquisite pleasure to see the smug cat-with-cream look slip from Catty's mirror-face. Nuria watched her discover that the pink didn't suit her, that it clashed with her coppery hair and bleached the color from her face.

Catty pivoted on the stool. "In your closet there used to be a blue dress that would be perfect for the Snow Queen." She looked back in the mirror as though realizing that pale blue might not suit her either. "It had little pleats."

Nuria thought of the dress, torn and stained, the back side shredded fine as corn silk. "If," she said, "seven maidens, with seven fingers each, worked for seven solid years, still they couldn't fix it."

"Pardon?" said Catty.

"In a word," said Nuria, "ruined!"

"Ruined!" said Catty. "But it was my fav—"

"There, there!" said Nuria. "Don't fret. Bertha's made a costume for the Snow Queen."

"Maybe I could mend it," said Catty.

"I never thought to see my Nuria sewing," said the Avy, pulling at a lock of Catty's hair in a tentative, teasing way.

"Sewing," echoed Mr. Winter, in a slow, puzzled voice, reaching for an embroidery hoop on the parlor table and setting it in Nuria's lap. "You used to love working on this."

Nuria stared at it as though he'd handed her a black widow spider. Half the oval frame was filled with tiny neat stitches that made a pattern of roses and birds. The other half showed a bare printed pattern of the same.

But she rolled the needle experimentally between her fingers. Embroidering would be stretching her good-girl imitation of Catty to its limits. "Not even you could mend that dress, O nimble fingers," she said to Catty at last. "Anyway, it was almost my shroud."

"Shroud!" said Mr. Winter, shocked. "Don't even think such a thing."

"Oh, let's get on with Pidalo Pom," said Nuria, suddenly cross, and held out her fists. "I hope I win the part of Gerda."

Catty put out her fists, and Nuria looked at their two sets of hands. Just a few weeks ago, she'd never have guessed that the short thin fingers that used to belong to her would be boxed into fists and turned against her own self as enemy.

> Elyn Glen, Fernway Fen.
> Ab-bey-bur-agh.
> Loch Oldlore, Blackhedge Moor. . . .

But Nuria's memory was her own even if the hands she held out were not, and these borrowed hands recognized the pouncing tap of the Avy's fist as it moved from girl to girl. The dance of Pidalo Pom was engraved on her memory and nothing could take that away.

> Cliffs of Murr-agh.
> Pidalo pom. Pidalo pom. Pidalo pidalo pidalo pom.

The Avy tapped Nuria's fist on the final "Pom."

"I won," said Nuria slowly. The Avy had let her win, but if she was Gerda in the play, that meant Catty wouldn't sing. Little alarms of shock ran down her arms and legs.

Catty folded her arms against her chest and glared. "I want to play Gerda."

"But you lost," said the Avy. "Fair and square."

"It's freezing in here," said Nuria fretfully, and wrapped her arms around herself. She couldn't stop shivering. She looked at Catty, at odds with her new face in the rose-colored silk, and it came to her slowly that the green dress Bertha had made for the Snow Queen wouldn't suit Catty any better. Maybe the dress would be an excuse to swap parts with Catty without Catty's becoming suspicious.

"But you'll look gorgeous!" said Nuria, remembering how the Avy had already worked on Catty's vanity once today. "Bertha's making you a beautiful Snow Queen dress. So, Minstrels! Strike up the band and convey us to my chambers. This maiden must examine the dress at once!"

But it was the porcelain doll Catty examined first. She flew to the bed, where the doll sat propped against the pillows. "Look at her tiny boots," she whispered. "They even lace all the way up!"

"Do you like her?" said Nuria. "She was for Christmas."

"I don't have anything nice anymore," said Catty, her hand hovering over the candy-floss hair. "Your Avy just gave me those eight little reindeer he'd carved."

"The ones in the Christmas window!" said Nuria, stricken all over again. How she loved those reindeer. "Well, here's something nice you can have."

The Snow Queen's dress was a shimmering mass of light green silk. Catty held it up against herself, pinching its shoulders to her own, looking down to see the silver smocking and the flounces of silver lace.

"Try it on," said Nuria. "Don't you think the color looks like ice?"

Catty wore a cotton union suit beneath the pink dress. "Oh for scrumptious, soft underwear," said Nuria. "I hate these scratchy petticoats."

"I don't," said Catty, slipping on the dress.

The silk slithered and rustled as Catty spun about, then curtsied. "Hmm," said Nuria. "The dress is beautiful, but a little big. Or maybe it's that the girl wearing it is a little small. Either way, why don't you take a look for yourself?"

The room expanded when Catty swung the door closed, enlarged by the reflected slice of room in the mirror behind it. Her face grew solemn as she stared at herself. "I look sick."

"At death's door," said Nuria. "It's not the best color for you, but don't expect me to wear it. I won the part of Gerda fair and square, just as the Avy said." But then she made her voice go so soft and wondering she almost fooled herself. "I hope the Avy's made that apricot dress so it will fit me."

"Well, he didn't," said Catty, smiling her cat-with-cream smile. "It's all made to my size."

"Despair!" cried Nuria suddenly, making Catty

jump. "Frustration!" She cleared her throat with a few little fake coughs. "Plans foiled and all that. What will you give me if I let you be Gerda?"

"I don't have anything to give you," said Catty.

"Oh yes you do," said Nuria. "Promise you won't ever sing with the Avy. I'll find out if you do and break your little fingers."

"We don't ever sing," said Catty. "I told you, I'm shy about singing in front of other people."

Nuria banged her fist softly on her knee. How stupid she was! She wanted to take it all back, tell Catty she could sing with the Avy, sing all she liked, just as long as she sang! But she was afraid her desperation would show through, and then Catty might suspect.

"That's just dandy," said Nuria lightly. "But we'll practice your song every day when we rehearse, and by next week you'll be ready to sing in front of everyone!"

Nuria had watched the Avy and Catty arrive from her post by the window, and she watched them leave the same way. Osa refused to leave with the Avy, and he had to fasten his belt around her neck. Nuria smiled fiercely when Osa pulled back against the makeshift leash, and she laughed when Catty slipped on a patch of ice.

This made Nuria think of skating, and of her brand-new metal skates. Catty wasn't using her skates, was she? Did she feel part of the ice when she skated, like Nuria? But that was Nuria's own special thing! In a burst of sudden fury, Nuria slapped her palms into her lap and hit the embroidery hoop. She took a deep breath. That was the test. If she could sew, Catty could skate like Nuria. If she couldn't sew . . .

Nuria poked the needle through the cloth. "At least they're small," she said, examining her stitches, which looked like tiny, unrelated ants on a vast, white plain. "How did this thread tangle all by itself?" She tried to pluck out what she'd done, biting at her bottom lip, and the whole thing grew into a jungle of knots and snarls. She tossed it to the table and laughed.

The parlor clock chimed the hour. "Hush!" said Nuria. "Can't you let even a minute pass without counting it?"

But the clock just ticked on: *Two weeks left, two weeks left.*

The half-hearted snow had slipped closer to rain. Heavy white water fell from the sky. Nuria no longer felt like laughing, for although she couldn't see the moon, she knew it was getting smaller and that in two weeks there would be nothing left at all.

The Revels

Nuria had grown accustomed to waking up to the smells of poached egg and marmalade, followed by the thump and rustle of Bertha's heavy steps and brisk skirts. But the morning after Catty's visit, the footsteps were wrong, light and tentative, although the smells were still the same. Nuria squinted her eyes open to see Mr. Winter setting a tray on the end of her bed.

"Oh, Bertha," she mumbled, grabbing for the porcelain doll. She liked to pay attention to it in front of Mr. Winter. "You look so different without your cap."

"That's it exactly!" cried Mr. Winter unexpectedly. "You are picking up more and more of Nuria's ways. Many of them have a certain charm, I'll admit, but when it comes to your embroidery . . ."

Nuria was really awake now. "What about my embroidery?"

"It almost broke my heart to see what you did to it yesterday. And as hard as you'd worked on it, too! You'd never have ruined it before you met Nuria."

Nuria had a sickening premonition of what was

coming. "It was an accident!" she cried. "Nothing to do with Nuria at all."

"Nevertheless," said Mr. Winter, "we've decided it best that you and she not play together just now."

"But the Revels!" cried Nuria. "We have to put on our play!"

"To be sure," said Mr. Winter soothingly. "You'll be together at the Revels."

"But we have to practice! How can we put on the play if we don't practice?"

"I should say," said Mr. Winter carefully, "that you'll be together at the Revels as long as you show us you can conduct yourself properly. Miss D'Estuffier is all for returning to Abbyburgh at once, you know."

A remark about Miss D'Estuffier sprang to Nuria's lips, and she bit it back down. She was afraid to say anything in case it sounded too much like Nuria. She nodded and clasped her hands together, and following the example of the porcelain doll in her lap, stretched her lips into a fixed and heavy smile.

The thaw continued through the week, and by the day of the Revels, mud and slush were everywhere. But under eaves and trees, where the sun couldn't reach, there remained fragile sheets of ice, thin as dragonfly wings. All week long Nuria had tied good-luck knots into her hair and smiled her porcelain smile. The knots mostly fell out of Catty's sleek, straight hair, but something must have worked, for now Mr. Winter was pushing Nuria through the big double doors of Town Hall, where the Revels were about to begin.

The great stone chamber felt colder than the outside. There was no warmth in the slanting oblongs of light that fell through the deep-set mullioned windows, and Nuria wished she'd let Bertha talk her into wearing an extra petticoat. She smoothed the green silk skirt over her knees, then with her fingertips stroked down the flounces of silver lace. She'd never worn such a beautiful dress.

She hung over her knees for some moments, feeling the blood pool in her head, her eyeballs so full she saw little sparks and squiggles. It was fun to feel the rush of blood away from her head when she swung up. She still saw squiggles, but now they were squiggles against an apricot background; and even before her vision resolved itself, Nuria knew it was Catty, wearing the apricot dress.

The Avy had made the dress beautifully. It had a shirred bodice and puffed sleeves, which were dotted with tiny rosettes of gathered silk, and on Catty's hair sat a wreath of gold roses. Nuria's cheeks smarted as though she'd been slapped. Catty twirled around, and the ruffled skirts glinted with reflected light, changeable as peacock's feathers.

That's my dress, thought Nuria, as she bumped

across the uneven flagstones, through alternating slants of light and shadow. She waited for the familiar surge of anger, satisfying and invigorating, but even though she'd had so much practice hating Catty, it never came. Her worry that they hadn't rehearsed Catty's song ruined everything.

By the time Mr. Winter settled Nuria beside Catty on the stage, Catty was standing quite still, looking over the rows of chairs below. They were empty except for the front row, where the village fiddlers had just taken seats and were scraping their chair legs about to find level spots on the craggy floor. Nuria remembered the fiddlers from last year's Revels. They'd played at the end, with the chairs all swept aside for dancing, and the Avy had bowed to her and said, "Madam, may I?"

The door opened again, and Miss D'Estuffier rustled down the aisle, the caps on her sleeves flapping, a waterfall of lace trembling at her throat.

Nuria nudged Catty. "Miss D'Estuffier must be furious," she said. "She doesn't show it, though. I behaved so well she didn't have any reason to say we should go back to Abbyburgh, and I guess she couldn't think of any more lies to tell your papa about me."

"I hate her!" said Catty. "I'll never let her marry my papa."

"You may not have a choice," said Nuria. "I can't be this good forever, you know. And then your papa will think she was right about Abbyburgh, and *poof!*" Nuria exploded her fingers into the air. "Catty Winter will have a stepmother after all."

There was a little commotion at the door as Mr. Garvey strode in crying, "Make way for the Golden Tenor!" Mr. Winter stepped over to close the dirty-gold stage curtains. "Aren't we lucky we're the very first act?" he said.

"Give me my props," said Nuria in a sudden panic. "Quick!"

Mr. Winter handed her a felt hat and a crown made of silver paper. Nuria put on the hat. "I'm pretending to be Kai when I wear this hat."

"Shh!" said Catty. "The audience will hear you."

"Let them hear," said Nuria, who was really speaking to the Wishing Well, hoping it could hear through the thick stone walls.

"When I'm pretending to be Kai," she said, whispering this time, "I'll pull this cloak over my shoulders." She demonstrated by pulling at the collar of a gray cloak that hung over the back of the wheelchair. "But I'm really Nuria. I'm Nuria all the time. You're smart enough to understand that, aren't you Wishing Well?"

The silver paper crackled in her hand. "And I'm pretending to be the Snow Queen when I wear this crown and my green dress." Nuria wound up the music box, but not all the way because she didn't want it to take too long to run down, and she held onto the winding key, keeping the music prisoner until the right moment.

The Avy peered out between the curtains, then glanced at his pocket watch. "Now!" he mouthed, and the curtains pulled apart, their tassels gathering a quantity of dust as they trailed across the floor. Nuria let go of the winding key, and the melody of "Darling Johnny" drifted into the air.

The villagers sat here and there in the great hall, filling no more than a quarter of it. It felt funny to see so many white and gray heads together, with Miss D'Estuffier as the bright exception. Nuria saw in a flash what the Avy and the others were afraid of. Without the families, the village was dying, truly dying. Nuria's palms were sweaty, but when she rubbed them together, they made a dry, papery sound.

"I am the Snow Queen," she began, "and I fly from window to window. Once I frightened little Kai when I peeped in." She waved through an imaginary window. "I make the ice freeze on the glass into beautiful patterns like flowers."

Nuria put on the felt hat and flipped the cloak over her Snow Queen dress. "I am Kai," she announced. "Gerda is my best friend, and we play in our rooftop garden."

Catty ran onto the stage. Her shadow followed her on the side curtain like a giant bat. "Oh Kai!" she cried. "Look how beautiful the roses are!"

Nuria put a hand to her eye and another to her chest. "Ouch! Something struck my eye, and now it has struck my heart!" She looked beyond Catty to her shadow, magnified and distorted against the curtain. "You look ugly and stupid, Gerda! I won't be your friend anymore." She slipped off the cloak and put on the silver crown.

"Kai got a bit of the demon's mirror in his eye," she said in her Snow Queen voice. "It made him think that pretty things are ugly. He also got a bit of the demon's mirror in his heart, which turned his heart to ice. I think that I shall steal him and take him to my palace."

The first part ended with Gerda sobbing and vowing to search for her friend Kai. There came a great applause when Mr. Winter closed the curtains for intermission, and then, to Nuria's surprise, the contents of her head shrank slowly away from the walls of her skull, and the stage receded into its corners. She leaned over until her forehead rested on her knees.

I'm not going to faint, am I? she thought. What an idiot!

Mr. Winter's clean, spicy smell came up behind her. "Let's get you some air."

He settled her on a window seat, struggling for a moment with the unfamiliar window latch, and then the out-of-doors flooded the little recess. The weather smelled of a sharp contrast, of the old stale snow of winter mixed with the muddy promise of spring. Nuria felt suddenly happy and hopeful.

The pale sky was overlaid with smoke; it was beginning to rain and the trees were black and wet. The Avy came up so silently behind her she might not have known he was there except for an elusive smell that alerted her, some combination of wood smoke and sawdust he wore wherever he went.

"See, Avy. See how the trees have feathery fingers?" The Avy stepped to her side. "It looks as though they're playing with the clouds."

The old familiar feeling of rightness rippled down her spine, and she laughed aloud with the intense pleasure of the describing game.

Nuria was so finely tuned to the presence of the Avy that she felt the sudden stillness as he held his breath. She turned to him; her eyes met his. He was staring at her steadily.

"Won't you take off your coat and stay a while?"

Nuria could not speak, but the Avy knew that and held up his hand. "I underestimated the trickery of the Well, but I'll never doubt my instincts again. I know you're Nuria. I know it down to the marrow of my bones, and the Well won't trick me now. I'll get you out of this somehow, you'll see."

"Time for Act Two!" cried Mr. Winter, which made them both jump; and despite what the Avy knew, Mr. Winter clearly thought Nuria was his daughter and that he had the right to scoop her into his arms and carry her back to the stage.

Act Two belonged mostly to Catty. Nuria sat beneath dangling tissue snowflakes, which meant she was in the Snow Queen's palace, watching Catty circle the stage in search of Kai. Catty made a good Gerda, Nuria had to admit that. Catty spoke so naturally, as though she truly felt every word she said. How could she be frightened to sing, yet find it so easy to act? Listen to her now.

"I see a palace made all of snow. Is that where I shall find my friend?"

Catty was circling the wheelchair, pretending to battle the biting winds that screamed through the palace. Nuria sat still and stiff, pretending to be Kai, frozen by the Snow Queen. But she could not pretend her heart was frozen. It would not listen to reason but banged about in her chest, pumping her blood into a boil. Her forehead was damp, and she could feel the heat rising to her face.

"Kai! Little Kai!" cried Catty, flinging her arms around Nuria's neck. "Have I found you at last?" Her cheek was next to Nuria's, and Nuria felt the hinged workings of Catty's jaw as it opened Catty's mouth. Surely it would come, it had to come, that first note of "Darling Johnny," vibrating into the bones of Catty's face and then into the air.

Catty peeled her cheek off Nuria's to whisper. "My throat's gone all tight."

"Just find your own note," whispered Nuria. "Pour it out, like gold!" She opened her own mouth as though that would help Catty, feeling so much a part of Catty's struggle that she merged into Catty. She felt how dry Catty's mouth was, so dry with fear that her teeth were gummy, and she heard the slight stick when Catty unclenched them.

"I can't do it," whispered Catty. "I just can't."

And here, where Nuria could justifiably have gone faint, she found her mind working fiercely and efficiently. In this state of Catty's, confused and frightened, paralyzed before an audience that was beginning to make itself heard in little rustles and whispers—in this state she might have forgotten that all the world thought she was Nuria.

"Show your papa you can sing!" hissed Nuria, taking this desperate chance that Catty wouldn't remember everyone thought she was Nuria, that everyone knew Nuria could sing. "He'll never marry Stuffy if she was wrong about that."

Catty took a deep breath.

"That's it! Remember your own special treasure, then pour it like gold from the glass cathedral of your head."

An eternity passed as measured by Nuria's thudding heart. Catty glanced at her father in the wings, then poured her song toward him, and Nuria wondered for the first time if Catty had missed her father.

> And it's where have you gone to, my friend, my darling?
> Where's your spirit gone roaming, my darling, my ain?
> They say that the maid from the city's bewitched you:
> How I wish you'd return to your own self again!

Nuria's jaw turned to water with relief, her tongue lay drowning in her mouth. She thought of her own voice and poured it out of her head, where it rang through the hall like crystal chimes. "I take it back!" she cried. "Do you hear, Wishing Well? I take back my wish!"

The strangeness began at once. She felt herself sucked long and thin, unbearably compressed, as though she were being drawn through the eye of a needle. This was not like the last time, a gentle transition through colored smoke. No, this was a . . .

"A snatching back!" Nuria tried to say, but her jaws had been ground to powder, her tongue pressed flat as a leaf.

She was expelled with great force out the eye of the needle; and when at last she found her breath and could open her flattened eyes, she found that her knees were pressing into the floorboards, her eyes staring into Catty's. It took only a moment for those transparent green eyes to register what had happened. Nuria saw Catty's pupils dilate into gleaming black mirrors, reflecting Nuria's own true copper-haired self.

Nuria did not look away from Catty, but her fingers

crawled up her sleeve to investigate an unaccustomed heaviness. Ah, the silken rosettes. She shook her head in rapid shallow movements. The wreath of roses shifted slightly on her head.

"Good-bye," she whispered, and looked away from her reflection in Catty's black-mirror eyes. With one finger, Nuria rubbed the apricot silk into her forearm. She imagined she could feel her blood beneath the silk, her very own blood, pulsing beneath her skin. She examined her short, thin fingers, then flipped her hand to look at the inside of her wrist. There were her own blue veins, visible reminders of the larger and wonderful network that ran through her whole body.

Catty cried out then, and Nuria's attention snapped from the marvelously ordered miniature universe inside her to the enormous and disordered universe outside. The Avy and Mr. Winter rushed onto the stage from the wings, and the villagers who, during Catty's song, had sat still and silent like so many butterflies on so many pins, now took to the air with a great murmur and scraping of chair legs. Miss D'Estuffier's bright head separated itself from the others and began to move toward the stage.

Nuria flung her arms around the Avy and rubbed her cheek into his scratchy shirt. Beneath the smoke and sawdust smells were more smells she'd forgotten until just now, a smell of the oil the Avy used to polish the clocks, and a whiff of the vinegar he used to sponge his clothes between washes.

"You're back!" said the Avy, holding her tight. "You did it all yourself. Oh Nuria, I've missed you so!"

Nuria put her lips to the Avy's ear to tell him they must be together always; but it seemed her tongue had a life of its own, for everything came out at once—how she loved him; how she'd made the wish-gone-wrong; how she'd waited for Osa in the snow, on Christmas night; how she hated the porcelain doll, even that. She knew that the meaning of her words blew about like a leaf in a storm, but the Avy did not stop her. He listened patiently, making his own sense of this gale of talk, guessing perhaps how sweet it was to say it all at last.

She was interrupted by a shout from Mr. Winter. "You were what!" He knelt beside the wheelchair; Miss D'Estuffier stood beside him, pressing her lips tightly together.

"Wish-gone-wrong!" cried Mr. Winter. "Marriage?"

Catty was also telling everything at once, mixing together her stories so they'd never come apart, like colors swirled into paint, pointing now with a trembling finger at Miss D'Estuffier.

"Ridiculous!" snapped Miss D'Estuffier. "Scandalous!" She whirled round and walked down the stage steps to the hall. The tumult quieted, and the villagers turned to watch. Her heels clicked loudly as she walked down the aisle to the great doors, which she pushed all the way open in her fury. The last thing Nuria saw as the doors swung slowly shut was Miss D'Estuffier turning neither to the right, which would take her to the shops, nor to the left, which would take her to the stables, but across the cobblestone street, sacrificing her leather shoes to the mud on the Common as she started down the embankment and toward the Wishing Well.

Mr. Winter's Wish

It was only February, but the trees had already blossomed in Bishop Mayne's magical early spring. Nuria stood at the edge of the Common, watching the lemonade light of early evening seep through a lacework of tiny florets. But night was waiting to take over. The moon was already rising, pasted against the sky like a round, yellow cheese.

"A coin for passage to your heart's desire," said Miss D'Estuffier. "That is the first rule."

Ha! thought Nuria. Greedy old thing! That'll teach her to make a wish for more wishes. This was the first time Nuria had seen Miss D'Estuffier since the day of the Revels, which was also the day Miss D'Estuffier became the Well's new Guardian. Osa pricked up her ears at the sound of Miss D'Estuffier's voice, sniffing in her direction. "How does she smell?" said Nuria, sniffing too, but she caught only an early-spring whiff of mud and sharp clean air, mixed with a trace of tar, faraway and therefore pleasant.

"One wish each lifetime; one cycle of the moon to repent and call it back. That is the second rule."

There came also, through this new, raw air, the sound of a hammer. No, the sound of two hammers. More than one family, newly returned to Bishop Mayne, was taking advantage of this early thaw to set its house to rights. The birds were singing a new song, and the frozen pond was breaking up, shuddering apart from itself, so that the whole of this spring symphony was conducted to a background drumroll of cracking ice.

The families had returned to Bishop Mayne. At least the Well was fair, Nuria had to admit that. When it revoked her wish, it had also reached further back in the chain of wishes and made the Avy's wish go right. Nuria was dizzy trying to explain it to herself. If a wish-gone-wrong makes another wish go wrong, but that second wish is revoked, the first wish is then set to right.

"And for that cycle of the moon, your lips are locked in this: To no one may you speak of your wish. To no one but to me, for your wish is my wish too. That is the third rule."

The grass of the Common had turned a brilliant green, that startling green of springtime that seems to come overnight as though painted with a huge emerald brush. It was also soggy, as Nuria discovered when she leapt down the embankment toward the Well.

She had nothing to say to Miss D'Estuffier, so she scrambled up the Well, which seemed smaller to her now. Had she expanded on her journey into Catty's body, or had the world shrunk? The cottage had also seemed smaller when she returned, and so did the Avy, although her arms still fit around his middle in the same way.

She smelled the roses first, heavy and sweet, then the damp coolness of granite. The hummingbirds were in flight, coaxing the very air into song. The blackness began to sort itself into grainy, quivering bits of gray. "Your eggs have hatched!" whispered Nuria, and she felt a sharp longing to pick up the baby hummingbirds, no bigger than honeybees. She curled her fingers into her palm.

"No grabbing!" she told herself sternly, sounding just like the Avy.

"A coin for passage to your heart's desire. That is the first rule."

Nuria slid off the Well and swung around. She'd already smelled the salty, hardworking smell of horse, but still she started back when she saw the horse's powerful shoulders coming at her.

"One wish each lifetime; one cycle of the moon to repent and call it back. That is the second rule."

"Too muddy for the wheelchair today," said Mr. Winter, sliding to the ground. "You'll have to stay up there, Catty, so hold on tight."

Nuria squinted up at Catty in the saddle, but the last of the setting sun dazzled her eyes, and all she could see was a dark figure outlined with fire.

"And for that cycle of the moon, your lips are locked in this: To no one may you speak of your wish. To no one but to me, for your wish is my wish too. That is the third rule."

"Most worthy and forgiving Nuria," said Catty. "Please accept my humble apologies for all that has gone before."

Nuria bowed graciously. "Accepted." She and Catty had worked out an agreement. From now until the next year's Revels, Catty had to say those very words every time she saw Nuria. After that, maybe she'd have apologized enough for keeping Nuria's body when she could have revoked the wish.

"Except," Catty muttered, as she always did, "I was going to revoke the wish anyway."

"Then you should have told me so!" said Nuria, saying what she always said, too.

Mr. Winter stood holding his hat as Nuria had so often seen him do, turning it about by the brim, waiting for the girls to finish. He made a shallow bow to the Well's new Guardian. "It's too bad you made that silly wish, Miss D'Estuffier."

Miss D'Estuffier sniffed. "Don't waste your pity on me. I can speak of nothing but matters of the Well now."

"Oh, it's not that I care about you," said Mr. Winter, so politely it took Nuria several moments to hear the sting behind his words. "But now you're stuck here, in the chair, in my beloved village until someone else makes that silly wish, and I can't bear the thought of seeing you every time I come to town."

"Someone could wish her to be free," said Nuria.

Mr. Winter held up his hands as though warding off a blow. "One wish at a time, please."

"Anyway," said Nuria, "she might stay in the village after she was free, just like Agnes."

Agnes was living in the rectory now, and doing odd jobs about the church. She had nowhere to go, she said, for she'd been Guardian so long that her farm was overgrown with brambles, and all of her children were dead.

"Then let's stick to making the wish we planned," said Mr. Winter. "Are you ready, Catty?"

"Ready," said Catty, but her voice curled up at the end in an unready questioning sound.

"I have a secret password for you when you get your legs back," said Nuria. "And also an invitation." The sun had sunk below the horizon, and Nuria no longer had to squint up at Catty. She saw how tightly Catty gripped the pommel, her hands doing the work her legs couldn't do of keeping her in the saddle.

"Do you have the coin?" said Catty.

Mr. Winter answered by holding up the wreath Catty had worn the day of the Revels. The roses shimmered into scarlet and crimson, reflecting the setting sun. Deep purple flooded the east, and the huge, round moon might have been a storybook picture of itself, dangling low in the sky.

"That's your coin?" said Nuria. "The wreath!"

"It's round," said Catty. "And gold."

"I suppose so," said Nuria doubtfully. "But it's mine, isn't it?"

"It need not belong to Catty," said Miss D'Estuffier. "But it must be precious to her, and she must have brought it."

Mr. Winter took the wreath from Catty. "We brought some more conventional coins too. Shall I simply, er, toss this in?"

"First I must tell you the rules that govern the making of this highly irregular wish," said Miss D'Estuffier, echoing the very words Agnes had once said to them. "Should you repent of this wish and want to take it back, both you and Catty will have to revoke it together. It is, after all, a wish that involves the two of you."

Mr. Winter bowed coldly.

"Toss it in, then," said Miss D'Estuffier, and cast a tendril of green smoke on her knitting needles.

Nuria held her breath and listened. The wreath struck the water with a dull thud, and as though she were an actor in a much-rehearsed play, Nuria found herself mouthing Miss D'Estuffier's next line.

"It has been found acceptable. You may make your wish."

Ribands of green smoke flowed toward Catty, looping around her in gauzy swirls. Light was draining from the air, emptying itself into some hidey-hole behind the sky.

"I wish," said Mr. Winter, then hesitated, and his nervous fingers strayed to his mustache. But there was no question that he knew what to say. It had taken six long evenings for him and the Avy to come up with this handful of words. Just twenty-one in all. Nuria had counted.

"I wish," he said again, "that Catty's body would now be what it would have been if she hadn't made her wish last year."

The smoke was thicker now, simmering with little bubbles and shivers into something deep and dense. One moment there sat Catty, veiled in gauze. Then the smoke-curtain closed, and she was gone. A scream came from behind the curtain, shrilling high and panicked.

"What a fool I was to leave her sitting on the horse!" cried Mr. Winter.

"It's scary to be in all that smoke," said Nuria, which made her remember the feeling of her body drifting off in swirls of gray and copper. "Ouch!" she cried, as though she'd been pinched. "I can't ever make another wish, thank goodness." Osa touched Nuria's hand with a cold nose.

The roiling smoke seemed to be getting paler, although that might have been the effect of the twilight, which drew the colors into itself as it deepened. "I wonder if Catty will be able to make another wish."

"Never say so!" said Mr. Winter. And then, curious, "What can you mean?"

"If she's going back to the way she was before her wish, then she'll be a person who hasn't made a wish yet. So she'd still have her wish."

"Oh, my Lord!" said Mr. Winter, striking himself on the brow with the heel of his hand. It looked funny, this theatrical gesture coming from the formal Mr. Winter, but Nuria had no desire to laugh.

"Probably not," he said in a voice more hopeful than decided. "She did make a wish after all." But he shook his head as he tried to work this out. "It's devilishly tricky."

"If she can make a wish," said Nuria, trying to be comforting, "she could wish for Miss D'Estuffier not to be Guardian. And if she does it right away, then probably Miss D'Estuffier would have somewhere to go, not like Agnes."

"Ooof!" said Mr. Winter, as though he'd been struck in the stomach. "Do me a favor, there's a good girl, and don't mention this to Catty. Look!" he cried, as though it were a relief to change the subject. "The smoke's fading!"

The time had come to see if those twenty-one words had worked, and Nuria deliberately made her eyes relax their focus. She couldn't bear to discover the whole truth at once. The horse's teeth and the whites of his eyes shone through the falling dark. Then a small flutter, like white doves released at dusk, made her sharpen her gaze. It was Catty's hands which, no longer needing to grip the pommel, had flown into the air.

Nuria laughed aloud, and her own teeth were shining as she cried, "Now you can be the scout, and spy out enemy territory!"

"Onward to Broomarium!" cried Catty, and waved her arm as though she were brandishing a sword. The horse skittered to the side, and Catty lurched forward.

"Careful!" said Mr. Winter.

There was no color left. The grass had turned to pearl. But Catty's face and hands shone in the moonlight as she urged the horse to a trot.

"Off she goes," said Mr. Winter.

"She might really go off," said Nuria. "Onto the ground, I mean. Isn't she the show-off!" But she said this affectionately, waving her arms at Catty, who was already wheeling the horse around and trotting back.

Catty slipped to the ground. "Look at me!" There she stood, her hair tousled, her freckles very clear in the moonlight. Her face was thinner than before, and she was taller than Nuria. Nuria hadn't expected that.

"Look at you!" said Mr. Winter, and picked her up and swung her around.

"My turn! My turn!" said Nuria. "I have to tell her our secret password." She handed the horse's reins to Mr. Winter. "Here, you hold these."

"Two headstrong girls," said Mr. Winter laughing. "I can see I'm in for trouble now."

Nuria stood close to Catty, smelling the new outdoor smell of her, and took her two hands. "I have a new name for Broomarium," she whispered. "Lace Dappled Grove. You remember the lace shawl?"

But she did not need to explain. "Lace Dappled Grove," said Catty. "Beautiful!"

Nuria tugged at Catty's hand, and of one accord, they went spinning round, connected by arms and hands, leaning out from the spinning center of their feet, infected by the magic and the mystery of the moon. Osa leapt about them, barking madly, as round and round they went until their fingers slipped apart and they collapsed on the soggy grass.

They lay side by side, Nuria's arm flung over Catty's. The moon hung so low Nuria felt she could almost touch it, and she remembered how she seemed bigger, how the world around her seemed to have shrunk. The hammering had stopped, but a smell of tar still lingered in the air. Very softly, Nuria began to sing.

> My love took me a-walking,
> In the purple dawn;
> Through the lace be-dappled grove,
> By the spotted fawn. . . .

She stopped, waited, and Catty joined her.

> My love took me a-walking,
> In the purple dawn. . . .

Their voices floated up to the moon, lost in the purple vault above. Nuria slid her arm down Catty's to find Catty's hand again.

"The Avy and I want you to come to dinner tomorrow, early enough for the singing time. The Avy said you might win at Pidalo Pom, and what would Miss Grabby Bones do then? But I told him not to worry about me. I told him that a princess wouldn't mind!"